BREAKING FREE

BREAKING FREE

Neha Nayak

Srishti
PUBLISHERS & DISTRIBUTORS

Srishti Publishers & Distributors
Registered Office: N-16, C.R. Park
New Delhi – 110 019
Corporate Office: 212A, Peacock Lane
Shahpur Jat, New Delhi – 110 049
editorial@srishtipublishers.com

First published by
Srishti Publishers & Distributors in 2016

10 9 8 7 6 5 4 3 2 1

This is a work of fiction. The characters, places, organisations and events described in this book are either a work of the author's imagination or have been used fictitiously. Any resemblance to people, living or dead, places, events, communities or organisations is purely coincidental.

The author asserts the moral right to be identified as the author of this work.

Printed and bound in India

To God, grandparents, parents, family, friends and my adorable pets -
Thank you for giving me selfless love, guidance and care.
You all are my life and mean the world to me.

My inspirations –
Dr A.P.J. Abdul Kalam, Naveen Patnaik, Ratan Tata.

Bachendri Pal –
I learn the sense of determination from her that no matter how tough and high the goal is, you have the power to achieve it if you think that you can.

Enid Blyton and Anant Pai whose books got me addicted to become an ardent reader and explore the world of stories.

Acknowledgements

I want to thank *each and everyone* who I have known and am yet to know – only for your presence in my life, I have gathered memories and experiences, and I am what I am today.

To my *mentors, idols, teachers* – for teaching me the elements of life and building me.

To my *organisation* – for supporting and motivating me to achieve my goals and set further ones, because "Improvement is a never-ending journey towards excellence".

To the *world of writing* – I have a long way to go in learning, enriching, improving and contributing.

To the *readers* – Thank you for picking the book. I will look forward to your feedback.

My debut book, like the first of anything, is and will be the most memorable and cherished. Thank you *team Srishti Publishers* for helping me achieve my dream of holding my 'first book'.

A few amazing buddies who had a role in the accomplishment of the book – *Ankita, Saurav, Abhishek, Binodini, Kokila, Rahul, Chintu, Ritu, Ria, Sonu, Sneha, Rani, Appu, Vicky, Deepa, Gayatri, Arjun, Sidhant, Appu, Riky, Pallavi, Seema, Sony, Prabhjyot*. Thank you and soon, I will again buzz you with my next ;)

Prologue

An year-and-a-half ago, I was like any contemporary young woman - having dreams to make it big, possessing the ardour to learn and developing myself to achieve those goals. My confidence was much talked about. In the beauty and fitness regime too, I wasn't behind. It took repeated turns for the gym instructor to come with a flushed face and say that I have worked enough. I was just like any girl in her twenties would be – looking at the mirror multiple times in a day, dabbing make-up to look prettier, posting all those selected photos on the social websites, and pursuing my hobbies. I have a wonderful family and circle of friends who stood by me, no matter what. I had a life which one ought to have.

But soon, my world came scattering down. That was because of one wrong decision, followed by another right decision. It was just a call, but a crucial one which shattered me to the core.

I stood in the hustling and bustling Howrah station on a cold and still night in the midst of a milling crowd, as I awaited my destined train. Minutes ticked by and I saw the train approach like a majestic giant – long, undefeatable, determined. Soon it halted with a loud screech. Momentary evil-ish suicidal thoughts crept in and tempted me to jump on the tracks and end it all, but a voice deep inside me echoed – *I'm not a loser. I'm not a fool. I love my life. My family and friends don't deserve this.* Now I faced the hour of truth. It was now or later. It is often seen that when it comes to personal experiences, we have been tuned to procrastinate things. But I had no time to delay my decision.

I decided – It was *now*. After all, they say, 'No one knows what's in store for us tomorrow, so live in the now.' It is only now that is under your control. Tomorrow is dependent on what you choose today.

I boarded the train and found my path, sandwiched amongst the passengers trying to fight their way to the train door. As I climbed into the train, I gasped for breath and searched for my seat mentioned in the e-ticket flashing on the screen of my mobile. On reaching it, I shoved my rucksack on the seat, spread the moist bedsheet given by the railway staff, and lay down on it. Fluttering my eyes, I turned my head towards the window and wondered again whether I had made the right decision – that of going away from him. Should I have given him a second chance? Could he have reformed? As such questions crept in, a sudden sporadic pang of guilt stormed and flashed through my shivering body. The train whistled and with the start of the train, my new life began too. I told myself when things are not in your control, it's best to move on.

Through the window, I only saw darkness – black, stubborn, directionless. Then suddenly, in the vastness of the dark night and tracts of land, I saw a small stretch of land lit up by shining bright sliver of the moon and a dangling lantern outside of a hut. Next to it was a cow standing in the midst of the barren land. If the cow had the strength to survive in such adversities, I could too. If the people in the hut could toil hard to keep themselves alive, I could as well.

I turned away from the window and looked at the other passengers travelling on the train. This is the real world – everyone living with a purpose. Life is never stuck at one place and is never at a standstill. You choose to perish if you hook on to a still time-frame.

It was then that I told myself, "Yes, I took the right decision. It had to be this way."

In the near past, I had been living my life in a limbo, without any goal or motive, just passing through time like a living cadaver. But now, I would live it my own way, moulding it the way I like.

As I swayed to the tune of the whistling 'chhuk chhuk' train, I remembered my good old school days when I used to get so excited to board a train to begin my vacation. It had been a long time since I had travelled in a train. Recently, lounges at airports where I'd wait for my flights were places I'd frequent while travelling – a result, both of India's dynamic growth and my position as the sole daughter of an affluent businessman. Today, I had chosen the train journey, where my childhood had its roots and where memories had been made. I knew I could fly high only with my roots strong.

Nostalgia enveloped me. I missed my parents, Neena and Shakti Agnihotri. We were Marathi but our generations, long settled in West Bengal, made us more tuned towards the Bengali culture. I assumed that by now they would have found their twenty-four-year-old daughter's 'adieu' letter. I felt guilty, but I knew deep down that what I was doing was necessary for me – for my inner calm, peace and strength.

"Breathe in and breathe out. Everything will get sorted soon. Life will be alive very soon. Have faith in God." I told myself for the millionth time.

Then I closed my eyes and sank into deep introspection, which is one of my favourite pastimes. It was only due to these interactions with myself that I was now on this train and wheeling off to a far off destination. Suddenly I put a stop to my pondering. I didn't want to remember the day that had passed. I struggled to shut my eyes tight and sleep. I didn't feel sleepy at all – not even a wink of drowsiness, even after an hour-long effort. The uneasiness within me was killing my peace. Also the thoughts churning inside my mind were volcanic. They could erupt anytime, because I hadn't vented it out earlier. I couldn't have shown a sulking face to my family as I loved them way too much to even show a tear on the face they cherished so much.

Suddenly, I felt the need to cry out, to release that pressure inside me. So I climbed from the lower to the upper berth and shielded myself by drawing the curtain of the berth, pulling a bedsheet over me. I finally allowed myself to cry. I gave in to the moment. I needed to sink in my tension through the unstoppable tears rolling down my cheeks. It was relieving me. I felt better.

The train halted at the next station and I could hear some passengers boarding and some getting off at the stop. Someone moved the curtain of my compartment a bit and I heard a male voice, "Excuse me ma'am, you are in my seat." Without moving, I replied, "Do you mind exchanging seats? Mine is the lower berth."

"Alright, that is absolutely fine with me," he said. "Who doesn't want a window seat?" I heard him mumbling to himself.

Subsequently, I heard him settling down, and then the sound of him logging onto a MAC laptop and a short phone conversation during which he informed someone that he had boarded the train and that he had had dinner as well.

A few minutes after his telephonic conversation, I heard a chuckling and giggling sound. It was high-pitched and irritatingly continuous.

After a minute of pause, again…then a minute of silence… then again…

The hyena-like titter was weird and funnily awkward enough to stop my tears and bring a stir to my face. It reminded me of all those hilarious scenes of actors which I saw on the television channels, You Tube, social media and movies. This was similar. I pursed my lips so as not to laugh out loud. I put a hand on my mouth and looked down to see what he was up to. I needed to make sure that he was not insane and that I was safe alone in the compartment with him.

The man was sitting on his seat wearing glittering white earphones and watching some video on his laptop. I decided to tell him that his laughter was too loud. So I called out to him but he could not hear me. When my attempts proved unsuccessful, I threw a bottle on the floor hoping that he would look up and I would manage to talk to him and apprise him of the disturbance he was causing to his fellow passengers – though in the compartment, it was only the two of us.

Thud.

The mineral water bottle fell onto the floor. But he just lifted it up without any prospective expected reaction, and placed it on my seat near my legs without even looking at me. My plan failed. I was too exhausted to climb down and talk to him or put any other strenuous effort to catch his attention. It has also been seen and proven in history, that if the mind is weak, even a bull's body will make no difference.

I got another idea and unwrapped the stole from my neck and dangled it all the way from my fingers down to the laptop keyboard.

Bingo! He looked up. "Hey, are you asleep? Your dupatta has fallen down." But he was shocked to see me holding and letting it hang down intentionally. I saw his eyes – deep black, alive, assertive.

I gestured to him to remove his ear phones and told him, "I can only sleep if you stop laughing so loudly." There are times when your mind is already so preoccupied with commotion that you can't take an ounce more. Today was such a day for me.

"Oh oh, I'm extremely sorry that I disturbed you. I will take care. You can go to sleep now. I will try my best to control my chuckles tonight," he said.

"Thank you. You better do that and not bother your sleepy co-passengers," I said while dilating my eyes to strongly emphasize the point. My tone sounded rough but I preferred to retain it that way.

Fortunately, I fell asleep in the next ten minutes. It was a major achievement for me considering that in the last few months, I had been struggling with insomnia. I woke up the next morning, once again greeted by the annoying chuckles and titters. I didn't have the composure to go through the ordeal again. I told myself that my destination was just an hour away so I will be out of the place soon. And so I decided to tolerate it with what God has given me – patience, perseverance and determination.

I reached Puri – the land of the Lord of the Universe, Lord Jagannath. I wanted to take the blessings of the Almighty God. I just had a rucksack, so I climbed down conveniently from the train, after jostling through the crowd in the train and the station. And suddenly, while I was walking towards the exit of the station, I heard a loud thud. Many heads turned towards the one who had just fallen down. Poor fellow. I ran towards the spot where the sound had come from. Someone had fallen down on the platform along with a whole lot of his luggage – one big airbag, one big suitcase, and a big backpack. I saw that it was a man and could only see his back. He was touching his head to check for injury perhaps.

I rushed to help the poor guy. That's me; I always stepped forward to assist other in need. I used to actively take part in many social volunteer activities as they added purpose to my life. I called out to him and held my hand out to help him. But he didn't see it, so he did not acknowledge it, and instead, put his hands on the ground and levered himself up.

"These days people don't value help. What a pity. And one should carry only that much which one can hold comfortably," I uttered to myself while retracting my extended hand.

And as he turned, "Oh, you," he said with a frown and the expression didn't look appropriate on his chiselled, handsome face which was covered in a beard. I noticed him for a brief moment; he looked like a model straight out of a fashion magazine. Any girl would jump to the sky and return, to go out on a date with such a good-looking person.

"You again!" I could sense the steeliness in his voice. His behaviour was unsuitable for a guy who looked as well-bred and decent as him. But these days looks can actually deceive. When you see the photographs of good looking thieves or thugs, you end up wondering how he can be one at first place and then the second reaction is of hatred on how he wasted his life.

"Yes, it is me. But why are you so annoyed to see me here? You are making me feel as if I owe you millions and am on the run from you," I said.

"On our first meeting you had problems with my happiness – my laughter which is cherished by my family and friends. What should I expect from our second meeting? As if that was not enough, you are now after my harmless bags," he said with displeasure.

"Well, an emergency is the reason of our second meeting. I rushed here to assist you after you fell down. And being a guy, what is the need to carry so much of baggage? That too when you are in trains and on railway stations. If you travel alone with so many bags, you are bound to slip and trip," I said callously.

"Who on earth said that guys can't carry a lot of luggage? I mean…I mean if all the girls out there can plan and carry outfits for every occasion, why can't we guys do it too?" he said without any warmth in his tone. A part of it also could be blamed to the bad hard fall he had had just a few seconds ago.

"I'm a girl but am I carrying a lot of luggage?" I said, raising my voice and turning to show him my red and black rucksack.

"Ma'am." His voice had taken on a belligerent stride. "Why am I defending myself? Are you my granny? I don't owe you any explanation."

He had raised the pitch of his voice to match mine.

"Excuse me. Do you know that you are very rude," I said irritated and shocked at his manners.

"Isn't it brutish to talk to me in that manner at a time when I have just escaped death? I could have fallen onto the bloody tracks. I got saved by an inch. Thank God." he said. "Where are the kind and mannered fellows these days. People are ready to fight with anyone on the road – just to vent out their internal frustrations."

"See, even I don't want to waste my precious time arguing with you. I'm leaving but before I do, I want to give you a bit of advice – If you are so careless then carry less luggage to avoid falls. This time you have been lucky. Life and fitness are more important, so focus on safety first, and then on fashion and grooming," I retorted.

"Oh god! There you go again. Goodbye. I have a long way to go. I can't get stuck here to take part in an irrational and illogical conversation," he said while settling and lifting the luggage with his hands.

I turned and steered myself though the milling crowd and I could hear a faint sigh from him and then…

"Rubbish! To hell with her. She looks so decent but see how rudely she speaks. Such a crude girl. Looks do deceive."

In truth, I did feel there was no rational reason for me to fight with that fellow. I was maybe, as he said just venting out the frustration within me. For a moment, I thought I should run back and apologize, but I didn't feel like it. The cold devil inside me won over my trifling warm emotions.

I hired a taxi to the hotel where I had booked a room. I spent the entire day in the tactfully decorated cottage room, sitting in the lawn, reading a novel, taking short naps, sipping coffee while admiring the heritage paintings of temples and the scenery around, watching TV for the sake of passing time, browsing on the phone, this and that. I managed to pass the morning and afternoon. In the evening, I went to watch the sunset from the adjacent private beach. The skies were orange with stripes of silver, grey and red. It was a magnificent view and I surrendered my senses to it. I breathed swivels of fresh air of freedom. I could feel the cold wind gushing and brushing against my body.

I felt that the blue wavering sea waves were calling out my name. *"Noya…Noya…Noya…"* It had a hypnotic ripple effect and they seemed to be inviting me to submerge myself in their lap. I wanted to feel the water. I walked to where the bursting waves met the serene golden sand and immersed my feet in the water breaking near the beach line, standing strong and taking the support of the protective sand under my feet. I felt blissful, ecstatic, and angelic, it was like washing out all my existent pain and emotions. Then the next moment, I felt like crying. My mind was in turmoil with a blend of positive and negative emotions.

I returned to my room only when the coast guard whistled, warned and shooed everyone on the beach away from the waters as the moon had emerged and the sky had darkened. The tempting sea was now roaring like a monster that could eat up whatever and whoever came in its path.

I returned to the room and checked my phone which I had left on the white duvet of my king-size bed. I had many missed calls and text messages from home, which showed that all their attention, back at home, was on me.

I called up Mom and asked her about the situation at home. I told her that I was fine and that I was on this trip to be alone with myself. I wanted to rediscover myself and regain my happiness.

We had a deal that I would travel around and she would allow me that. In return, she would get my happiness, my smile and the real Noya back. My mother understood my need to travel, and it was she who suggested this plan when I had shared with her that I need some solidarity. She had then shared with me a secret – when she was in her prime days, before she met dad, she was in love with a police officer. But he being a Christian and she a Hindu, their families didn't agree to the relationship. And so, they had to call it off, as they didn't want to start an alliance without the blessings of the families. She was deeply heartbroken, and to relieve herself, she had gone on a pilgrimage trip all by herself. I had also shed tears on hearing her saga and thought about the numerous lovers who have had to sacrifice their love just for the sake of others!

My father knew that I'm travelling, but with my friends. My mother added a small lie and told him so, else I wouldn't have been allowed to travel on my own, given the state of my mind. She sounded relieved on hearing my voice and told me that I must take care of myself and call her every hour and update her. I agreed with a condition that she would not send anyone to keep an eye on me. I said I wanted to travel alone and I would return in a month. But I negotiated that I would call her every day as I felt I would lose my strength if I spoke to her every hour and would feel like returning home.

After the conversation, I logged on to my iPad browser and connected to the internet. I typed in 'Jagannath Temple Puri' in the Google search bar for information on the place. I have a habit of learning about any new place before I visit it so that I can get acquainted with it and be well informed before I am actually there. I slept well that night, excited to visit this temple of rich heritage.

The next morning, I woke up quite early and started for the Jagannath temple. After a fulfilling shrine darshan and relishing the delicious bhog, I left for the station to catch the evening train to Rameswaram in Tamil Nadu.

In the evening, in the train, I opened my journal and made my notes.

Places to Visit (Spiritual)	
East – Puri	✓
South – Rameswaram	
North – Vaishno Devi	
West – Shirdi	

After I settled myself on the upper berth, I began reading a novel. I was suddenly startled by some familiar titters. I looked down, only to find that 'train guy' again.

Oh god. Not him!

Can't I burrow a hole in the train and hide myself there. I prayed to god to turn me into a cockroach for a few hours for the act. I tried my best to remain unnoticed. But finally, nature's call defeated me. I had to get down to go to the washroom. I wrapped a stole around my face before I climbed down.

I returned and ascended up to my seat and heaved a sigh of relief. I managed to hide my identity in the similar manner the next day too. But the third day, an unexpected incident occurred.

When I opened my eyes after a nap in the evening, I saw the ticket examiner and that 'train guy' looking at my horrified drowsy face. Was I hallucinating? No, I was not.

I scrambled up and looked at them. The examiner asked me to display my ticket. I said that he had already verified it and again repeating it wound mean harassing the passenger. The guy then said that I had hidden and covered my face throughout the journey and all the passengers considered me a threat. This was horrifying to me yet quite necessary for others, considering that there were alerts scattered in big fonts in all the newspapers. But I knew I wasn't a terrorist. So what was the big fuss about.

"Lady, can you now show us your face, else I will have to call the police?" The fat train ticket examiner was under pressure from the fellow passengers. All my pleas, excuses, bickers went unheeded. Can't I kick the fatso on the place where it would hurt the most? But then, it was my problem and not his. He was just doing his duty.

I had to descend and after I did, I unwrapped the stole from my face, and then I heard a loud shriek and a squeak from that bratty 'train guy'. How I wished I could punch him and hit him hard to the ground along with the examiner.

The confused and convinced examiner left after the verification of the ticket and photo ID. The guy and I looked at each other for a long while and had a very awkward moment of silence. He broke the gaze when he realized it had been too extended. I wondered why I had been meeting him repeatedly. So frequently.

He did not bother to apologize and finally just murmured some words to himself and sat down on his seat. I gathered myself after the embarrassing incident and returned to my cursed seat.

After some hours through the night, the train came to a loud halt and there was no sign of movement for an hour. I looked down and out through the window; it was dark outside. It could not be a station as there were no lights. I saw many passengers getting down the train carrying their luggage. I realized there is an issue. I climbed down. The 'train guy' was sleeping and roaming in the tunnels of dreamland.

On inquiring I got to know that there was a breakdown on the railway track and repair work was on. It could take hours. Another passenger shared that Rameswaram, my destination was just half an hour from this place we were stuck in. I tossed in my mind – thirty minutes or hours. I chose the shorter one.

I disembarked with a few other people and we walked towards the nearest station which was five minutes away. The flashlight on the mobile helped us in guiding our walk. Modern day applications do help us in lessening the weight we used to carry earlier.

It was 2.00 a.m. when I reached the station. It was a small and neat one. The platform wasn't buzzing with people and I felt a bit apprehensive as I tend to get nervous in lonely places. But as soon as I came out of the station, it was even scarier.

Out of those very few people who were present, men fiddling with their big moustaches and ogling scared me all the more. The ones who were present seemed to be weeding as I could see smoke and also smell the affected air. I looked straight, right and left, and stood in the middle of the road and pretended to be busy on my phone by vaguely tapping my fingers on it. Then out of nowhere, I heard the buzzing sound of an auto rickshaw, and I saw the 'train guy' on the opposite side of the road, sitting in a black and yellow auto. Never in my life had I felt so relieved. I felt like running up to him, hugging him, giving him a kiss of gratitude and asking him to accompany me. But my ego was holding me back. I saw him approaching me, waving at me, and soon he was standing right in front of me.

"Are you all alone here too? Do you want me to accompany you to your hotel? You, see it's not safe here," he asked.

Hotel. My mind rang sirens of alertness. Why does he think I'm heading towards a hotel. It could have been to a relative's home. It could have been another railway station to catch a transit train. What does he want to do with me after reaching the hotel? Beware Noya. You can't give him strands of hope that you are available for one-night stands! I did hear from others every now and then how such escapades don't have a baggage. After the encounter, he goes his way and you your own – no strings attached. But I was the type who only vouched for long term relationships. My thoughts were interrupted as I saw him waving his hand. Of late, I had become too judgmental. Too quick to arrive at conclusions. I was having a hard time trusting people.

"No, I'm fine. I will manage on my own. I'm used to such travels and scenarios." I said curtly. Gosh, did I just say that… at this hour of the night when in reality, I had never travelled in such a secluded place alone ever?

"Think again, this is the only auto rickshaw I could find after walking a while towards the end of the dark road. There are no street lights there, there are urchins on drugs and streets dogs," he explained, sounding genuinely concerned.

"No, I'm fine. You carry on," I said. What was I saying when I knew that if he would go, I'd be all alone.

"Okay, fine then. Reach your place soon, else spend the night on the platform of the station and leave for your place in the morning. The platform is safer than the road," he said and left in the auto rickshaw.

As I watched him leave, I could hear my heart thumping and screaming at the blunder I had made. My palpitations only increased their pace with every passing second. I was back at the pavilion of insecurity. I looked around in all directions trying to get a taxi or an auto rickshaw, but there were none in sight.

I switched on the GPS on my phone and started walking towards the main road, but it didn't catch up to show the location map. The internet was very slow to use any applications to book a cab or an auto. I wondered where the promised 3G or 4G network was. How the advertisements on the bill boards and televisions are just a hoax. When you really need them, they just don't work. I was in a fix. How could I have been so lax by not arranging transportation beforehand? I again thought of him. If he could get an auto, why couldn't I? I started walking towards the left. After some fifty-seventy steps, I heard some nocturnal sounds – hoots, howling, whispers…

I ran for my life. One thing which really scared me was darkness. I recollected the day when once, during a school camp in a wild-life sanctuary, I had followed a deer to capture its video and had got lost in the jungle. It started to grow darker with every passing minute. I stood at the spot, clueless at which direction to move in. But seeing the sky turning dark, I prayed to god and ran helter-skelter, not stopping till I reached a hut. That run of my life had saved me.

I rushed back to the station and to the platform now hosting very few people. I seated myself on a vacant bench and recollected that guy's words: "*…else spend the night on the platform of the station and leave for your place in the morning.*" It made sense to me now. Only if I had taken his offer to drop me to my destination.

Shouldn't I have accepted his offer to accompany me? My thoughts were interrupted when I saw two weird looking drunkards approaching me. One had graying hair and the other a deep scar under his right eye. I looked away as I didn't want the encroaching people to know that I was attentive to them. I thought they would go away but soon, they were so near and so drunk that I could now smell the alcohol in the air. They couldn't even stand upright. Both were swaying while asking me, "Auto, auto. We also have deluxe taxi."

"We have air-conditioned one for a beautiful madam like you. It will be a pleasure and a safe ride for you."

I said 'no' and turned to the other side to avoid them. By then, they were standing near me and were pulling my bag and saying, "Please come, we will drop you. It is not safe here." One of them had called another person and had started speaking to him. "We are coming with her."

I shouted loud enough, "No! I don't want your damn auto and stay away from me." I also started typing the emergency police contact number which was displayed on a board in front of me.

"Madam, we are trying our best to help you. Why are you feeling we are bothering you? Come with us now," a man said with bounty of liquor smell coming from him. He came nearer to me and pulled my purse.

Bang Bang. What followed was the learning into action. All that I had learnt in the self-defence class was my saviour. I overpowered him with a fierce blow on his stomach with my elbow and kicked him on his leg, smashing him to the ground. Seeing this, the other man ran away.

"What do you filthy people think? You can get away from anything?" I said while calling the typed number and informing the police.

"Hey, so you are here! Shed your ego and come with me, else such perverts will harass you through the night."

Waves of relief flushed through my quivering stomach when I heard this familiar voice. Soon the police arrived and took the demented person away.

"Oh, so you are brave. I saw you giving that punch and kick. What strength you have! I was lucky that I didn't receive a blow that day I fought with you at the station." He said while raking his hair through his fingers. Under the lamplight, his face dazzled like a Greek god's.

"Ok, now follow me. Enough of perils for the day." He said in an authoritative tone, which can be reciprocated with no questions, no arguments, just discipline.

I smiled but didn't utter a word and dubiously followed him straight through the station to the auto rickshaw. There are times when you must let go of your ego – in love, in relationships, at the workplace, and for your safety.

As we sat on the seat of the waiting auto, I asked him, "Why didn't you leave? And why did you come back?"

He said, "I had left my wallet in the shop from where I had bought a bottle of water before I left the station, so I had to come back all the way to get it."

The auto rickshaw driver commented, "Why are you lying, boss? Ma'am, he was actually very worried for you, so after a minute of commuting, he directed me to come back to the station and started looking for you on the road. When he didn't find you there, he got more worried and went inside."

We shared a long, awkward, silent journey after this. Sometimes you just have to stay quite because no words can explain what's going on in your mind and heart. We reached the nearest decent looking hotel – it was three-storied with paint peeling off the walls, but we checked in and took two adjacent rooms as there were no other hotels nearby. And we didn't want any more adventures in the middle of the night. There had been enough already.

I thanked him before going inside my room and fell into a deep slumber after a tiring, rollercoaster of a day.

I woke up to the music of chirping birds, the hide and seek of sunlight streaming through my window. I felt energetic and looked forward to the day. This is what nature offers when are out of air-conditioned, sealed rooms and houses. I got ready, checked out of the hotel, and left a note for the 'train guy' at the reception informing him that I have left for Rameswaram, suffixed with a 'Thank You'. On the way, I had a scrumptious breakfast at a nearby restaurant. I always raved about authentic South Indian food. On any South Indian friend's wedding, I didn't leave the dining hall till I gobbled on at least four servings of food.

I proceeded to the Rameswaram temple, renting a cab from a travel operator's office. The temple architecture was magnificent and stood unconquerable. There were twenty-two holy wells inside the temple and as per ancient holy scriptures, one should take a dip in the water from each well to get the blessings of the almighty, to wash away one's impurities and sins, and to gather strength and courage.

I witnessed mythology that I had heard about from my grandmother and read in stories. I had heard that the stones here are porous and so they float in the water. A shopkeeper selling those stones demonstrated it with his wares. I saw the bridge which Shri Ram had built to reach Ravana's kingdom to rescue Sita, and the holy Sanjeevani-hosting stub which Lord Hanuman carried to save Laxmana's life. It was a pious and spiritual experience. Seeing historical wonders which you only had heard before, is exciting, simply amazing and unbelievable.

In the evening, I boarded the train to Delhi. From there, I had to travel to Katra and then to Vaishno Devi. I opened my journal and updated it.

Places to Visit (Spiritual)	
East – Puri	✓
South – Rameswaram	✓
North – Vaishno Devi	
West – Shirdi	

As I started reading Sophie Kinsella's *Shopaholic to the Rescue* on my tablet, I was interrupted by the familiar and annoying chuckling, this time coming from the adjacent compartment.

Are you kidding me! It was just not possible that it could be him again. Life does have coincidences, but this seemed highly unlikely. It can be anyone else, but not him.

I was so curious to ascertain my doubt that I got down from my berth and peeked through the curtain of the next compartment. It was indeed him. Before he could see me intruding into his private space, I rushed back to my seat and covered myself with the bedsheet. I had not yet recovered from the previous night's embarrassment. I didn't have strength to encounter another ordeal with him. I blamed the frequent encounters to the algorithms on the railway ticketing software which has fixed compartments and seats for specific routes.

Victory! He didn't see me till we reached Delhi. I managed the game of hide and seek quite efficiently. I was pleased and patted myself on my back after I saw him exiting the station gate at Delhi.

The bus to Katra was just about to leave when a man hurriedly mounted it and the conductor directed him to the vacant seat next to mine. It was none other than the 'train guy'. All this while, our meetings had happened only on trains and now he was here in this bus too! Was it sheer coincidence or was he stalking me? Had he been sent by my family to keep an eye on me? I became very suspicious and was desperate to know what was actually happening. But I chose to keep quiet.

As he settled his luggage on the rack above the seat and sat down, he turned and saw me. His mouth went wide and he cried out, "Are you kidding me? Is this just a coincidence or are you stalking me? Have you been sent by my family to keep an eye on me?"

"Excuse me. Are you insane? You think I'm stalking you! As a matter of fact, you are stalking me!" I screamed back at him, forgetting all the help he had extended to me earlier.

"Chill. No point blaming each other. Let us talk and sort it out. I don't like public drama," he said, talking sensibly for the second time. It was then that we both realized we had been so loud that now the fellow passengers were eyeing us warily. Even the conductor's and the driver's eyes were in our direction. So he lowered his voice and hushed -

"I'm Ranbir and I'm on my way to Vaishno Devi," he said.

"Then where are your other friends or family members? Don't tell me you are travelling all alone," I said.

"If you can travel all by yourself to so many places, can't I go to Vaishno Devi? What's your problem? From the time we met, you have been eyeing me with suspicion and insensitivity. Just because I'm travelling solely and carrying a lot of luggage, you think I'm capable of blowing up a train or a bus. I have helped you in times of distress. So at least for that, you can consider that a friend in need is a friend indeed. But no…instead you have problems with my laughter, my luggage and now my itinerary too," he said.

"No. I'm no friend of yours," I said. "All criminals initially try to gain the trust of the victim and then show their true colours," I mumbled to myself as I covered myself with a stole.

"Excuse me? What did you just say? I am not a criminal. You will never change. It is good not to trust strangers, specially the reappearing ones, but you are really harsh in your words," he said. Before I could answer, he closed his eyes and fell asleep in a second; or rather, he feigned to fall asleep.

After a while, the conductor came to examine the ticket. After scanning my pockets and purse, I concluded that I had lost mine. He said I should give cash to get a new one from him but I had only ten rupees with me. I had forgotten to withdraw money from the ATM before boarding the bus. The conductor was a super grumpy fellow who did not agree to let me withdraw cash on the way. I damned my luck. My days were transitioning from a bad to worse phase. I sat there clueless, not knowing what to do next. He told me to get down and travel to Katra in some other bus after I withdrew the money. I had to get down from the bus with my bag.

At the bus stand, I tried to locate an ATM in the vicinity but I didn't find any. After scanning the surroundings with my eagle eye, at the three hundred and sixtieth degree angle, I saw one at a distance, and ran up to it with the hope that I could still withdraw money and get into the same bus on time before it left. But hard luck! I inserted my card multiple times, but every time, there was an error on the screen. Finally, I called the guard standing outside and he told me that the machine was out of order. I asked him for directions to another money vending machine. He said that the nearest one was five kilometres away. But that meant another forty minutes at least. He said that the bus would leave by then. And the next bus would be only after four hours. I started to panic. I took deep breaths to keep myself calm. With no other option, I called an auto and got into it to reach that nearby ATM. Just then, a hand stopped the auto I was in; it was Ranbir's! I was in a perpetual shocked state. I couldn't gather what was happening at that instance. Why was he stalking me so insistently? What did he want from me?

"Hey, girl. I dozed off but does that mean you can't wake me up? By now we have met a dozen times so god has something in mind for us. We have some sort of connection. You see, a connection of being human. I hope you feel the same. At least you could have told me of your situation," he said warmly.

"But I don't need your help. In fact, I have friends in Delhi. I will call them for help. You don't have to worry. I don't want to trouble you," I began, hardly looking at him.

"Oh god, stop it now. Follow me," he said in a reliable tone, while paying off the minimum rental amount to the auto I had hired.

I silently followed him like a student follows his class teacher. I felt so helpless and dependent that I wanted to kick myself on my butt for this temporary amnesia. How could I forget to withdraw cash? I'm not roaming around in malls, multiplexes and restaurants that I expect a cashless tour.

I boarded the bus and sat in my seat.

"Sorry Madam. Sir made us realize how insensitive we have been." The driver and the conductor of the bus apologized to me. I enlarged my eyes in anger but soon with a smile, forgave them.

I was an ardent reader of Lord Budha's philosophy. *'Hanging on to anger is like drinking poison; so let go'*. Let go. I remembered how I used to sit in my grandmother's lap and she would read out Buddha's noble eight-fold path. I opened a site and read it again -

1. Right View – is to see the world through the eyes of wisdom and compassion.
2. Right Thought – clear and kind thoughts build good, strong characters.
3. Right Speech – by speaking kind and helpful words, we are respected and trusted by everyone.
4. Right Conduct – no matter what we say, others know us from the way we behave. Before we criticize others, we should first see what we do ourselves.
5. Right Livelihood – choosing a job that does not hurt others. "Do not earn your living by harming others. Do not seek happiness by making others unhappy."
6. Right Effort – a worthwhile life means doing our best at all times and having good will towards others. This also means not wasting effort on things that harm ourselves and others.
7. Right Mindfulness – this means being aware of our thoughts, words, and deeds.
8. Right Concentration – focus on one thought or object at a time. By doing this, we can attain true peace of mind.

"Thank you." I whispered to the train guy.

"Always welcome," he replied.

Once again, he dozed off, or acted to. I don't know. He could be so kind and helpful but at the same time he could be so pretentious and act as though nothing out of the ordinary had happened.

I sat thinking of what I would say to him when I paid his money back, which I would do the moment I found working a money-rendering stupid machine. Then I napped for a while.

"Wake up, wake up," a voice called out to me.

I opened my eyes.

"What happened?" I asked while rubbing my eyes. My eyes take a while to get to normal vision after a nap.

"The bus has halted for lunch. Let's go and eat," he said.

"But why should I have lunch with you? I still don't trust you," I said.

"Holy god! What a girl. Madam, you can sit at another table and I will sit at another for your sake. Now let's go and eat something. The bus won't stop after this till it reaches Katra. And I have a lot of luggage. I can't carry an unconscious girl along with my luggage," he said with a grin.

"Excuse me! Okay…I will have lunch. Thanks," I said.

It was kind of weird that we only interacted when in distress or in need, as throughout the journey he didn't speak a word to me, nor did I. For a moment I wondered if this guy indeed was a stalker, the very reason I was averse to him.

On reaching Katra, I rushed to the nearest ATM with him. That is when I realized, after shoving my hand into my bag to take out my wallet and the debit card in it, that both were missing. Rekindling my memory cells, I remembered that I had left them in the ATM counter at the bus stand in Delhi. I was completely lost in an unknown land now. I did not know what to do. I came out and shared my plight timidly with him.

He was grave and silent for a minute, then stroked his dark black beard and then roared out laughing, looking as happy as a monkey who had received a banana. My problems seemed to be a source of entertainment for him.

"How could you? You are such a reckless and careless girl. Yet you are on a journey all alone. I don't know who you are, where you're from and where you're going. How did your family let you go all by yourself? Anyway, do you know anyone here?" he asked sympathetically.

Looking down at the wet ground with green grass, without lifting my head or looking at him, and with tears in my eyes, I answered. "No. My wallet had a precious group photo of me, my grandparents, parents and pets. It was an old one which we had taken when I was three years old. I just had one copy of it and it was in my wallet."

"You should always keep a backup of all such valuable photos," he said.

"I have, but this photograph had a message written for me in their own handwriting, from my grandparents and my mother. And whenever I miss them, I feel the photograph and it keeps me motivated. I get strength from it," I replied.

"I understand. I'm so sorry. Don't be sad. We will lodge a complaint with the police. I will take care of it. Just give me the details of your wallet. Hopefully, we will trace your wallet." He said so dismally, that for a moment I felt him to be my own and wanted to run to him, hug him and share my agony. I was not the type to open up so soon, but here, the dynamics were different.

"Hmm." I sighed.

"Tell me who you are now. I need to know about you since I will have to ensure you reach your home safe and sound. I have to make sure that I'm not steering any illegal activities through you," he said jokingly.

"I don't want to talk about anything personal with you. Rest assured that I'm not into any illegal trade and am not a terrorist. Here, look at my driving licence," I said while flashing it before his eyes. But I quickly put it inside as I didn't want him to note my address or parents' names.

"Oh, are you a secret agent who has been commanded not to divulge any information? Okay, it's fine if you don't want to share any personal data. But for now, just follow me," he said.

With no other option, I had to, without any protest.

We checked into a hotel. A part of me had begun to trust him. After all, in this journey, his was the most familiar face. I called Dad from my mobile and gave him an update on the journey.

"Yes, Dad. I have reached Katra by flight. I'm staying at the Taj. Tomorrow I will visit Vaishno Devi with my friends. Everything is fine here. You need not worry. And I will keep you posted," I said to him, a little guilty about the big fat lie.

I had been lying to him and telling him that I was on this journey with my friends. He is a very caring and loving father, such that every girl in the world would want. I missed him when I remembered how he waited for me to have dinner together every single night. How he sat awake till I fell asleep when unwell. He sat in the front row of the hall and cheered and clapped when I performed on stage. Tears flowed and the kohl amalgamated with it to fall on the pillow, looking like small polka dots.

As I lay on the bed and read an e-book, I could hear my stomach grumbling and growling. And there I was – a penniless, dependent, hungry traveller.

I sat cross-legged on the bed, closed my eyes, chanted Om, and tried to calm myself down and think about a way out. I usually do this when I feel my blood pressure is rising. I decided to call my father and divulge the truth. I would then have help right away. But my plan was interrupted.

Tring… Tring …Tring… Tring.

The phone in my room buzzed like an irritating, shrieking whistle.

"Hello. Are you planning to eat air or would you care to eat something edible?" Ranbir asked.

"Ah. But I …" I started and paused as I just didn't have the words to complete my statement. One hand was holding the telephone receiver and the other was holding my rumbling stomach.

"I have ordered some food for you. Vegetarian. It will reach you in ten minutes. Please eat and relax. I'm here for you till you resolve your monetary problems," he said.

"Okay. Thanks. And I am extremely sorry to bother you," I said. I hate to trouble anyone, let alone a stranger.

"Not at all. As long as you don't call me or think of me as a stalker, no trouble at all. I believe you have come here to visit the Vaishno Devi shrine. I'm going there tomorrow. So join me at 4:30 a.m. in the reception. I will be waiting. And anyway, you have no other option than to join me. I'm far better than the rest of the preying stalkers," he said laughingly.

"Okay. I will be there," I could hear myself agreeing. I did have an option, but I chose to be led by him. From tomorrow, I would be back to the life I came from.

"Can we introduce ourselves to each other now? Isn't it really strange that we have been meeting all these days and still we don't know each other? All that I know about you is that your name is Noya, which I accidently heard when you were registering yourself and checking into the hotel room," he said while we were ascending the slope of the mountain hosting the Vaishno Devi shrine.

Before he could say anything more, a grey-haired old lady from a group of pilgrims called out to us, "Hey there! Please join us. We are a group of pilgrims from South India. We don't know Hindi, so do you mind joining us and guiding us on the trip? This is our family."

Before I could say that this was also my first trip to the place, I heard an agreement between Ranbir and the group of pilgrims. And before I knew it, I was walking along the sloping pathway with the amicable family comprising three kids, three middle-aged couples and two elderly couples.

"Hello dear, are you friends?" asked one of the elderly ladies.

"No," I said.

They noted my crisp answer and shaken tone and looked at each other, trying to guess the relationship between both of us.

"Oh, brother and sister, then?" Another lady asked.

"No, no," Ranbir responded quickly.

"Husband and wife,?" asked an uncle this time.

I was at a loss for words and made my best possible attempt to avoid meeting the eyes of the pilgrims or Ranbir. But he was looking at me. I could see from the corner of my eyes but I did not want to look straight into them.

I was in such a dicey situation. I was with a close-knit family, walking towards the holy shrine and I could not tell them why I was with this guy. Could I be in a more bizarre and freakish situation?

"Uncle and Aunty, we are not close friends, nor brother and sister, nor a married couple. We are just good friends who have paired up to visit the deity together. You know these days, friends tag along only when you have to visit Goa, Bangkok, Las Vegas or some places where you can party hard. But here we are – two good friends who decided to go on this spiritual trip together," he said, trying to act over the shelf."

His unexpected response sent a chill down my spine, cutting straight across my heart. I got goosebumps ad I looked into his eyes and we exchanged a smile.

This was the first time that I could look at him, straight into his eyes. He had sharp features, a fair, chiselled body, a pleasant smile, kind eyes which were charismatic and appealing, yet so disturbing. My heart skipped some beats. His musky perfume felt soothing. Having shared space in confined places so often, by now I was familiar with this fragrance.

I was interrupted when one of the kids held my hand and steered me away from the thoughts about Ranbir.

The ambience of the Vaishno Devi shrine was exhilarating and intoxicating. All the pilgrims were chanting *'Jai Mata Di'* together. Some were holding hands showing unity. Some forgot their physical incapability and showed determination to reach the goddess. The journey to the shrine made me forget my own identity and worries.

In front of the shrine, I sought the blessings of the powerful goddess and prayed for forgiveness if I had hurt anyone. I just surrendered my past and asked for strength for a new beginning and for the life ahead. I instantly felt that my confidence and strength of mind had exponentially improved.

While returning down the slope to Katra, the family thanked, appreciated and invited us to visit them in Chennai.

After the family left and we returned to the hotel, we had a short discussion in the hotel lobby. He asked me, "What next? Where are you proceeding to? I'm going to Delhi. You come along with me. I will then book tickets to your home from Delhi. You are my responsibility now; since you have been with me all along, I can't leave you alone till you reach your home."

"I will go till Delhi with you, return your money and then we will part ways, if that is okay," I said.

"Why do you always sound like a hangdog?" he said and then looked at the screen of his tablet. "You look so forlorn, gloomy and woebegone," he said chuckling, reading out from the dictionary he had on the display.

"Excuse me. Out of all the adjectives in the vast and infinite dictionary, you found only these adjectives to describe me?" I said extremely annoyed.

"And out of all the infinite emotions in the world, why are you always so dejected?" he asked.

"That is because…wait, why am I answerable to you?" I said curtly.

"Okay. Get ready in thirty minutes. We have to catch the bus back to Delhi. I know you must be tired so you can rest your legs in the bus. I need to start for Delhi as I have an important meeting there. Else we could have started late after a nap," he said.

"And listen, I have friends in Delhi. I informed them of my plans yesterday. They will be there at the bus stand. I will return your money then and there, and then we will go our separate ways," I said, wanting him to know I was not as helpless as he thought. Also my curtness could be contributed to the warm feelings which I had started developing for Ranbir. He helped me every time I needed, and still I in no way could return the favour. This was driving me crazy even more.

"When did I say we would go in the same direction? I don't need the money, but I guess you are one of those egoistic people who can't sleep peacefully until they return the money they have borrowed," he said mockingly.

"Yes , I am. Good that you realized that," I said.

In the bus, I chose a seat far from his so that I didn't have to have unnecessary conversations with him.

As the bus came to a halt at the Delhi bus stand, I could see Rima standing with Rohan and Ayan. They were my best buddies, who had always been there for me through thick and thin. We were childhood friends.

While I got off the bus, Rima screamed, "Darling, why are you travelling in a bus? How did your parents allow you to travel in one?"

I ran up to her and whispered in her ears, "Dad doesn't know at all. Mom knows a bit. He thinks I have been taking flights and staying at elite hotels. That I'm not alone and am travelling with a group of friends."

"Alright, it is tough to understand you at times. Here is your money. You wealthy idiot, asking me for money. For a minute, when I got that text, I had a mini heart attack. I wondered if it was really you or if you were in some crisis. I was scared someone had kidnapped you and you were sending that text at gunpoint. And hey, where is that guy you texted me about?" she said, looking around for the train guy.

"Which guy?" Rohan and Ayan shouted in chorus. "What did we miss?"

"Hey, quiet, guys! I will share everything with you. For now, let me go to him and return the money and end all the emotional drama with him," I said to Rohan and Ayan while taking money out of the wallet Rima had got for me.

I saw him standing near the bus door. I ran to him like a scurrying mouse and handed him the cash.

"Bye, young lady. Though we did not talk much, thanks for your awesome company. It was really warm and cordial," he said sarcastically and paused. I did not know what to say to break his gaze.

"Bye," I finally said and ran to my friends. The adieu didn't feel comfortable as I had imagined it would be.

But I saw him standing there, with a very disturbing gaze that cut across my heart. What did his eyes want to convey? I distracted myself by looking through the other window of the red Audi car we were in, and went to Rohan's aunt's house, which was close to the airport. I changed my clothes from ethnic to a western outfit – a knee length navy blue jumper suit paired with red danglers and red belly shoes.

"So, what surprise have you planned, guys?" I asked. Rima had been dropping hints of a surprise to me the previous day.

"We are going to Shirdi and then Goa!" Ayan said.

"Shirdi! Wow. That is in my travel wish-list too. Thanks. You guys are my life. You all have been there for me at my beck and call, no matter what," I said. A sudden stir cringed my body when I thought of the love of my friends. On a call, my friends came down from Mumbai and Kolkata just for me. Rima left her boutique business for some days, Ayan his real estate business, while Rohan took few days off from his corporate life. Could I have wished for anything better than such good friends?

While I said 'good friends', I felt a shudder inside me, like a bolt of lightening. I looked around, almost as though I expected to see the 'stalker' everywhere I went.

The next day we flew down to Mumbai. In the flight, while I searched for my journal, I realized I had perhaps lost it at some point during the journey. I cursed myself for the transformation in me which had emerged of late. I had turned so careless. I wasn't like this before. I didn't appreciate this version of me, but I also knew this was temporary. Soon, I was sure to be back to my original self.

We proceeded to Shirdi in the car Dad had sent. My lonely trip, which wasn't as lonely as I had desired, was over. My parents were now well-informed about my whereabouts. I had also confessed to Dad about the trip I had travelled alone till now, unable to bear the lie I carried. They had even arranged for my luggage to be transported from Kolkata to Goa as now, I would be needing extra set of clothes and other necessities. I recollected that indeed, when you travel long, you would need additional accessories and attires. I felt bad at my behaviour which I had displayed earlier towards Ranbir. But he was gone now – somewhere else. I couldn't even apologize to him as I never bothered to seek any identity information from him. This was unusual. When he was not around, I felt like apologizing, yet when I saw him, all that I did was crib and bicker.

I felt at peace at the Shirdi temple. When I bow down, Sai Baba always gives me strength and rejuvenation. And with this, I ticked the last destination I had on my wish-list in my mind. I again sighed as my journal had my intricate details jotted in it. And now it would be lying in some garbage dump.

Goa – thronging with energy, throbbing with upbeat youngsters. Age doesn't matter. Everyone is a youngster here. One could be as wild as one wished. You can be all whacky, and no one would give a damn!

We had booked a two-storied exotic bungalow with a sprawling garden where you could pluck vegetables and prepare your own meal with the assistance of the butlers. At the front of the house there was a small flower-bed and lawn with a swing.

We would stay there for the next ten days. During a previous visit to the place, I had read an article in the newspaper where some children were rescued from a cracker factory. I was initially anguished at the ruthless owners for making the soft and small hands work so hard. In a subsequent article, the affected children had been interviewed and said they weren't happy with the factory closing down. For them, it wasn't a rescue. They wanted to work. They wanted to earn money for their living, for their family. That was when I had planned that I would open an NGO in Goa for under-privileged children. I wanted the children to feel empowered with education. It is only education that can reform societies and nations.

I called up Samaira, the daughter of my father's business partner and a long-time friend of mine, and asked her to join me for lunch that day. She consented. I got ready and drove to the restaurant.

There we talked about Samaira's escapades with her new boyfriend. I could see she was trying really hard to share crazy jokes and stories of funny incidents to cheer me up. I laughed and laughed…and the next moment, just cried aloud. I put my fingers over my eyes and bent my head to hide my tears from others. Samaira pulled me to her chest and consoled me.

She then took me to Joggers' Park and we sat there till dusk, looking at the active joggers, the still green grass, the trees and the distant sea waves. Peace, serenity and the soul always gel well. After dinner at Samaira's place, I reached our bungalow where my friends were waiting for me. It was 11 o'clock by then. After much persuasion, I agreed to play something. We played truth and dare, and after that my friends started drinking. I had never got drunk. Nor did I intend to today. We partied the whole night, dancing to the music till dawn.

I woke up the next morning with the constant buzz of texts and calls. Some were from Samaira updating me on the status of the ongoing infrastructure work at the school.

The institute was to be named 'Eme' an abridged form of 'Empower Me', with future plans of branches in Goa, Mumbai and Kolkata in the first phase of deployment.

Through his social contacts, Rajan Uncle had already selected the first batch of children to be enrolled in our program. There were sixty students enrolled at the Goa branch. We had arranged a bus service for these children, which would ply around the city and pick them up from their own or shelter homes. I decided that we would also provide the students with good food while they studied in our classes. I drew up the food menu with ample calories and all the required vitamins, minerals, proteins and carbohydrates. After all, how can one study attentively if he is undernourished? In addition, we also would give away stipend which would act as an inducement for the parents of the children to send them to school.

"Yes Uncle, I'm at Eme. The putty and painting work is almost done. You can send the furniture in the second half. And I have signed the contract for the meal today. I think we are in a position to start classes by next week. And don't worry, your daughter Samaira is managing it so well," I said to Rajan Uncle over the phone.

These days, I was trying to be happy. I was reinstating some meaning into my life – adding colour to my life which had got lost in my immediate past.

After supervising the ongoing masonry, garden and administrative tasks, I left the building and started the drive back to my temporary nest, which was to be my home for the rest of the days in Goa.

I felt so empowered. I was now free to follow my dreams. Useless relationships restrict you. You are always so preoccupied that you forget you have a life of your own. Life is not about eating, drinking, working, waking up to another day, only to live the monotonous routine. It's actually meaningful when you do something for one another. It's satisfying only when you do something what your heart tells you to do.

After an hour of drive on the road, I entered a lonely stretch.

'Brrrrrrrrrrrrrrrrrrr...Brrrrrrrrrrrrrr...Brrrrr'

Something was certainly wrong with my car. Its engine stopped midway on the deserted road.

Alas. I was on this lonely road with big residential houses all around. I could see no soul to help me, except for two street dogs that came close to my car wagging their tails. I opened some biscuit packets lying in the backseat and threw the biscuits to them.

I waited for twenty minutes outside the car but still, there was no one in sight.

This is the problem with exclusive and ritzy residential colonies. The watchmen and the residents are all behind big mansions hidden by trees. You can see no one there. Just roads between the columns of houses…long lonely roads!

When I lost hope of sighting any humans, I picked up the phone to call Samaira for help.

Oh God! What happened to the network on my phone?

"Useless phone. Stupid SIM. Idiotic network. You can't be out of reach now!" I lamented at my phone, while getting out of the car and standing on my toes in the hope that adding some height would get me a feeble signal. But it was of no use. Helpless and hapless, I stood there in that unknown place.

A big car rushed by me. Then it reversed and stopped near me. A man in his late twenties got down.

"Hey, miss, is your car giving you trouble?" He said.

"Excuse me," I said, still looking at my phone.

"Has your car broken down? Hello, I'm Ranbir. Not Ranbir Kapoor though. May I be of any help?"

I didn't know what to say. That voice was familiar. It couldn't be him again. He was clean shaven this time and dazzled with all his million dollar good looks under the bright sunlight.

"See, after I leave, your probability of finding another car will be one in one hour. And if you call up any other friend or acquaintance, they will reach here in one or two hours. You see, this area isn't close to the city. So decide soon and tell me. I'm going for an official meeting. I need to plan and inform the clients accordingly," he said.

"Yeah, okay. Actually I do need help. My car is not starting. And more than the car repair, I need to go to a washroom or else my bladder will burst!" I said squeamishly.

"Oh, I can understand. Once, when I was in the fourth standard I was in the playground and my sports guide didn't let me go to the washroom in time. And guess what? I peed in my pants!" he said.

"What!" I exclaimed.

I was shocked that on a lonely road, on a car misadventure, I was standing and talking to a partially known stranger and sharing pee mishaps. But after experiencing weirder incidents in the past, this was tolerable.

"Hello! I need to go to a washroom!" I said while pointing a finger at my stomach to express the urgency.

"Do you mind going to my house? It is just around the corner in case you need to reach a washroom quickly. But there won't be anyone there as it's kind of a recreation house. So I leave the decision up to you," he said.

"I think it would be better if you could take me to a shop or a restaurant nearby. Some public place which will make me feel safer," I said.

"Oh yeah, girls' safety. I can understand. I have sisters too. Moreover, you have it in your mind that I'm a known stalker so how can one trust stalkers however known they may be," he said with a smile.

How could the 'train guy' be here? I was now almost certain that he was a professional stalker. All my kind thoughts which I had developed for him earlier dissipated. I even had some ideas as to why he was stalking me – he wanted to kidnap me and then demand ransom from my rich dad; he wanted the land of my coaching institute to build some estate. Many more frightening motives came to mind.

I found myself asking, "Aren't guys supposed to understand all these, things with or without sisters?"

Pity this guy's girlfriend or wife, I thought.

"Can we go now?" This time I asked in a stern tone.

"Yeah. But let me push your car to the side of the road."

Saying this, he pushed the car while I steered the driving wheel.

It was then that I realized I would have to go with him in his car.

"See Ranbir, since you have sisters, you can understand if I keep the windows open, right?" I said as I seated myself in the passenger seat of his car.

As he started his big, black, elegant Jaguar, he said, "Yes, of course, if dust and grime is not a problem for you."

"It isn't," I snapped.

For the entire five minute drive, which seemed like a century with my full bladder, one of my hands was on the front door handle. I was all ready to jump in case of any mishap. And the other hand...well, it was inside my purse holding the pepper spray!

We reached the nearest restaurant in five minutes. I ran inside holding my stomach, took care of nature's call and came out.

As we drove back, he asked, "What's your name? I now want to formally get introduced. It is high time now."

"Noya."

"Noya. I know you are Noya. Noya what? And don't you think it sounds like 'Noah'. Like Noah's Ark. You must be feeling proud, Noya. Have you read the Bible?" he asked.

"Yes I have," I said without looking at him.

By now, I was acquainted with his lame questions and the even lamer jokes. I said to myself, just two minutes more, and thus calmed myself down.

When we reached my car, there were two men standing near it.

"Don't worry, they are car mechanics. I called them to fix your car," he said.

I gave them my car keys. My hand was still on the pepper spray.

In five minutes, they had repaired my car and it started.

"Thanks Ranbir. And please apologize to your clients on my behalf. I realize I have delayed your business," I said.

"Mention not, Noya. It's just being human. Bye for now. Hope to see you soon. And next time, do not get into a stranger's car and go to a washroom. I mean, do you have any idea how dangerous it is?" he asked, sounding like a counsellor.

While he was leaving in his car, and I in mine, I shouted back:

"You looked innocent and trustworthy today. Moreover, you are not a total unknown stalker, but a known stalker by now. And I always carry a can of pepper spray!"

How strange it was that I had been encountering this chaser so frequently? I kept wondering about this for many, many hours. As a result, the next morning, I woke up quite late. I stood in front of the mirror and saw that I had dark circles under my eyes which had also turned puffy. I had cried the previous night, keeping my head under the pillow. The pillow had got stained by the kohl I wore. There were little black polka dotted remnants of the kohl on the white pillow cover.

It was the day of the opening ceremony of my school – the much awaited day and the attainment of one of my most aspired dreams. These were my drops of happiness in the vast ocean of depression. My friends and I reached the place. Through the grill of the main gate, I saw that Samaira had already reached there, standing tall in a white kurta and churidar with a red stole wrapped around her neck.

As we entered the main gate, Samaira shouted: "Surprise!"

My father and mother emerged. For a moment, I stood there speechless, my mouth wide open. I pinched myself to ensure that what I was seeing was not a dream and then screamed, "Mom and Dad, thank God you are here! Today I'm so happy. Thank you, thank you, thank you for coming. I love you. You are the best! And what a surprise you have played up to. And you said you both have to attend another event so won't be able to attend this."

My mom is one of those women who is always immaculately dressed. She looks younger than her age and stands tall, unbent and pretty. She is the one I admire the most. Her strength, courage and judgment are always fair and square in all circumstances. Whenever we go out together, people mistake us for sisters.

As we waited in the area arranged like an open classroom, my students arrived in the big yellow bus. Dad had organized an inauguration function in secret coordination with Rajan Uncle and Samaira. I was amazed how all of them had managed to hide the plans, all under my nose. They had invited the Tourism and Education Minister of the state, Mr Aryan Mallya, for the ribbon cutting ceremony. And soon he arrived. A spotless, bright white SUV pulled up. First his armed bodyguards alighted, and then him.

And wait, was I hallucinating? Oh man, what was I seeing? Oh no, no, no....

Amongst the group of people surrounding the minister was Ranbir, dressed in a safari suit and accompanying the lanky minister, who wore clothes a size larger than his frame – a white kurta, white pants and a grey Nehru jacket. Now I was convinced that Ranbir was an employed spy and a professional stalker. I needed to find out who had hired him.

I went close to him and whispered in a lowered voice, "Listen, I won't tell anyone. Just admit this to me. I need to know. Was he my Dad who sent you after me?"

Just as he began to answer me, "I suppose..."

"Hey Noya, come here. Mr Mallya wants to meet you," my Dad called and interrupted our conversation.

With a grunt of despair and disbelief, I went up to him and greeted the minister, while glaring at my dad. I was angry and boiling over like a volcano that could erupt anytime. How could he do that to me in spite of all my requests and assurances that I needed time with myself? I had even said I was taking my friends along with me!

"Hey Noya, what a remarkable girl you are. What a noble thought to open up this institution. Good going. We need more of such young philanthropists in India. Only then our country will be truly empowered. Here, meet my nephew Ranbir Mallya, my sister's son," the minister nodded at Ranbir.

I couldn't believe what I was hearing.

Ranbir... Ranbir Mallya. My thoughts defied all barriers now. Had my parents gone insane? Now they wanted me to marry this leech. That had to be. That is why they had sent him after me.

Feeling vaporous with my blood pressure shooting up, I felt like Sherlock Holmes for having cracked the case. I went close to Ranbir again and whispered in his ears, "If you think I'm interested in marrying you, please know that I'm not."

He gave me a blank stare, smirked and moved two steps forward. I moved forward and brought my mouth closer to his ears and saw that they had changed colour from pale pink to red.

"Did you hear what I said?" I asked.

"Stay away from me else prying eyes will think you are trying to kiss me on my ears. We will talk later. Don't give anyone the notion that you are trying to flirt with me," he said.

"Kissing? Excuse me. You think I'm trying to flirt with you. Are you in your senses?" I said.

"Then you are crazy to think that I wish to marry you. I mean, look at you. You always look like a depressed and heart-sore lady. I have stated this to you earlier also, yet there's no change in you. And you've got this eccentric habit of jumping to conclusions," he said.

"Enough. You don't know how to talk politely. I don't want to talk to you. Especially now that I know your intentions," I said rudely.

"Who wants to talk to you! Am I the one following you here and there trying to talk to you desperately? It is you Noya," he said.

"Sir, even I don't want to talk to you. But I want to know the reason why you followed me throughout the journey, all the way to today!" I said.

"I wasn't following you," he said.

"You were!" I said.

"I can't help it if you don't believe me," he said.

"I don't believe you. I know someone has made a deal with you to stalk me on my journey. I just want you to confirm it. That's why you were there every time I needed someone. Earlier I thought it was sheer coincidence but now I know it is otherwise," I said.

"Bye. You are mad. What's your name? Yes, 'Noya'. Noya, know it…you are insane!"

He made an exit, leaving me in a perturbed and perplexed state. The most dangerous state of mind is when it is left in an open state with millions of doubts and suspicions popping up. I wanted to close the loop by getting to the root.

Mom and Dad left for Kolkata the next morning. On reaching home, Mom called and told me that Ranbir had called her to share that he had plans to help me with the social cause I was working for. He wanted to invest in a noble deed and had chosen mine. Now I had no doubt that my parents had intentions to marry me off to him. But then, this was a doubt I had. I decided to confront my parents, but only after being sure of this. How could they be so insensitive? My thoughts, my emotional trauma, my feelings were all still raw. They hurt every other minute, every now and then. However much I tried to forget and stay away from my thoughts – my heart, mind and soul defeated me.

But I was strong and so had managed to keep all this turmoil inside me. I did not want to appear disturbed and despondent in front of my parents and the world. I wanted to shield my parents from all the pain within me because it would affect and sadden them. All this while, even they were behaving as though nothing had happened. I wanted to shield myself from the world because I didn't want to seem vulnerable, neither did I want to seem glum. But what Ranbir had said to me did affect me. I had tried so hard to stand upright and behave normally, yet he called me a 'heart-sore' person. My internal dynamics was shaken. I can't just let it happen.

My thoughts were interrupted by a message on my phone.

"Hi Noya. Can we meet at 7.00 p.m. at the Café Regal? I hope aunty has briefed you on the purpose." It was a text from Ranbir.

"Okay, I will be there," I replied.

Ranbir and I met that evening. Rima, Ayan and Rohan accompanied me. I took them along to upset his plans of a marriage, and to let them see what kind of a stalker he was.

But he very wittily greeted all my friends, gained their regard with that refined behaviour of his, and then excused himself along with me for a short stroll along the beach on the pretext of some business talk.

While walking along the coastline, on the cold and grainy sand in the chilly seaside wind, I shivered and got goose-bumps.

He took off his coat and offered it to me. After some coaxing, I put it on. I felt warm in it. My heart paced its beats. My knees turned jelly again.

"So, Noya, I called you here to talk about business. I want to support your cause. I want to expand the portfolio. We can start vocational courses for different groups of people. Currently you only offer classes for children. I would like to expand those to include women, the old and the differently-abled," he said, sounding like an experienced philanthropist.

My thoughts sizzled, my hands trembled and my heart palpitated. Why was he doing all this? Did he have a soft and warm heart within that deceiving personality and two-faced exterior? Was he just helping me out of the goodness of his heart, or did he truly have a selfish motive?

I was constantly distracted by his gaze into my blinking and confused eyes. So I tried to avoid it by turning my head towards the sea.

"Ah, before we engage in a partnership, I want to make something clear," I finally said.

We were now walking on a granite track inside a small park on the beach.

My palpitating heart finally gained courage. I had to say this to him before his hopes soared high.

"Listen, Ranbir, before your expectations soar, I want to make it clear to you that I have only recently separated from my boy friend. And if you and my parents think I will marry you, please do away with those expectations," I said, turning my head away from him.

While talking, I hadn't been looking at where I was going, so I didn't notice a ridged stone in my path. Before I realized what was happening or could figure out why I was falling towards the rocky ground, I was caught by him and now I was lying in his arms – his face turned down to look at mine.

"Noya, I'm so sorry. I really didn't know about your break-up. Now that I know, I realize I should not be rude to you, but I want to be. You have a tendency to be humorously idiotic. How could you assume I was stalking you? And not only that, now you think I was stalking you because I want to marry you! I knew you are quick to arrive at conclusions without knowing facts. How many times should I say this; you have to change."

His expression when he said all this was far from calm.

We gazed at each other for a long time, only being alerted to our surroundings when a boy passed us by and whooped. After a while, I released myself from his hold and stood straight, straightening my displaced blue beaded necklace.

"Let's return to the restaurant and have dinner. Then go home and rest. I will meet you tomorrow at your NGO office and we can discuss our plans – professional, *of course."* He stressed and accentuated the 'of course'.

Back with my friends, the look on everyone's faces had turned rosier and all eyes were looking into mine asking a thousand questions. We had a big spread over dinner and Ranbir didn't let any of us pay for it, saying it's a treat for the business deal between us.

I dressed myself in a traditional manner – partly as I was going to my school and partly to look like a shattered soul. It's so strange that when you have a good mood, you don't mind utilizing all the time to look good and when the mood isn't right, you just want to look decent enough with the bare minimum effort.

I wore a light pink kurta and white dhoti pants – I wanted to look years older than my age. I have a set of such clothes to help me accomplish this trick when I need it. Otherwise I look years younger than my age, thanks to my genetic inheritance and my mother. She did really take good care of me and has passed on very healthy habits to be me – drinking milk, exercising, praying, meditating, and talking to my family and friends every single day. After all, these contribute in developing happy hormones and 'happy' is how life has to be lived. I put kohl on my eyes and a pale pink lip gloss.

I had been trying hard to forget my terrible past, but this man had refreshed and reloaded my memory cells and crashed all the confidence I had gained.

"No. I have to be strong. I love myself, my parents, my friends, my pets. I love the world. I love my life. I have to cope with it. For them. I will get through this. I can and I will," I said to myself.

Sixty children between six to eighteen years of age, with glee in their eyes and smiles on their lips, sat on chairs and rested their hands on the wooden benches. My friends and I distributed uniforms, notebooks, pencils and pens, school bags, educational books, tiffin boxes, and water bottles. The ambience soon turned noisy with their happiness in the form of chuckles and giggles.

One tiny girl with plaits, wearing a knee length frock came to me and said, "I want to fly to the moon." Her friends made fun of her asking her which human being can fly. She answered back saying, "I will. I will become an astronaut."

Hearing the aspirations of these kids, I felt a tumult of satisfaction. My nostrils flared and I felt tears of joy fill my eyes.

I introduced the teachers to the students. I gave a little inspirational speech to the students on how important and necessary it was for all of us to understand, read and write basic English and Hindi and to know and master a skill which could help them provide for themselves and their families. We had planned fun-filled activities, games and inspirational movies for the day. In the evening, during the recreational dance session with the students, I remembered that Ranbir was to come and meet me but he had not yet. I checked my mobile phone, but it didn't have any messages or calls from him. We were not such close buddies yet that I could text or call him to enquire why he hadn't turned up. Again my ego took over me.

The day passed with the kids and in the evening too, I didn't receive any communication from him. I felt that he must have been offended at all my baseless accusations and blabber. I felt that I should call him up and apologize, but I could not lift my fingers with my emotional strength. I didn't have the mind and the patience to get into another emotional battle – already one was simmering inside me. I wasn't ready to conceive another one. I preferred to keep the situation as it was. I would deal with it as it came.

That night, my friends and I sat playing 'Truth or Dare' on the terrace. In the very opening spin, the bottle pointed at me. I was made to sing a song. At the second spin, Ayan had to do a striptease and take off his shirt and vest, showing off his abs and muscles. Next, Rohan had to behave like a monkey and show us a banana eating stint. Rima was the one left and claimed to be the winner. The winner had the privilege to ask any one of us a personal question or wish in private. She chose me. She took me to the garden area. The seaside breeze was calming. We sat on the comfortable beanbags and talked.

Her question was, "Why are you such a deaf, dumb and blind girl to stick to silly emotions?"

Her wish was that I drink beer with her. After a lot of reluctance I did touch the most sought after liquid in the world, after water, for the very first time in my life. Though I hated the bitter taste of the spirit, I swivelled the big mug for her. We were soon intoxicated and feeling pretty high. Things around me faded out. The ground was spinning. The sky was restless.

"Noya, you are such a young and beautiful girl. Why are you spoiling your future by keeping yourself stuck with that brat? What a chicken he was," she said.

"Rima, stop. Let's not abuse anyone, however chicken they were," I said.

"A chicken should be called a chicken! Nevertheless how chicken he was!" she said.

"A chicken is a chicken always and forever and ever!" I laughed as I said it, then began to cry the next moment.

"I do remember that chicken most of the time but it was all destined to happen. I gave him so many opportunities to change, but he never did!"

"That's what I'm saying – he is a chicken," she said while puking on the ground. "He is a stale chicken that needs to be spewed and retched."

"Hmm… I don't know when that chicken will leave my thoughts. Good night, Chicken…wherever you are! Hope you are happy and at peace now after eating up my bloody heart and life! But you will never understand what love is. You just had some kind of obsession. It was not love. You must be sleeping peacefully. Sweet dreams!" I shouted at the top of my voice at the starry sky and the moon whose light reflected off the beer mug placed on the small round glass table beside my beanbag.

I lazily tossed, turned and got up. That was when the bell rang. Again it rang. I opened the door. And I saw Ranbir standing right in front of me with a flower bouquet in his hand.

"Here. These are for you. A work of origami by children of an NGO based in Delhi." He said while handing over the paper-work flowers.

"These are awesome. I will start origami classes in my school too. Look at this. Small hands and what creativity with perfection," I said while keenly observing the art.

I hurriedly then adjusted my hair and dress, and spluttered, "How come you are here."

"Yes, I'm here. Pinch me to see if it is me or some spooky ghost in my guise," he said.

"What are you doing in my house looking at my face, you spooky ghost? You are promoting yourself now, from a stalker to a visiting guest!" I said chuckling, trying to get as far from him as I had not yet brushed my teeth.

"Wait…wait..wait…hold on before you say something nonsensical and hurt me again. Give me a chance to speak today. Won't you call me in or you intend to finish the whole conversation keeping me out of your house?" He said while raking his hair. "Or are you cautious and ensuring that I'm not that serial killer newspapers are ranting about."

"Oh shut up! And I'm sorry. I'm just too stunned to give out a reaction. I hope you understand. And where were you yesterday? I was expecting you." I said allowing myself to release the emotions. "Come inside."

"I had gone to Delhi yesterday for a business meeting. And I went to the police station with a tiny hope that your wallet would have been found by some good-hearted, honest fellow and that he might have returned it to the police," he said.

"And…" I asked and paused, wondering what he would say next.

"And…" He paused. "I came to return your wallet," he said, taking out my long lost, precious wallet from his black and red backpack. "And your invaluable photograph is intact. The policeman said he tried your phone a couple of times but it was unreachable."

"Oh yes. I have kept my phone switched off and am using another one for now." I jumped out of the sofa in joy, hoorayed, went to him and gave him a quick, nearly imperceptible hug and thanked him repeatedly. I realized after doing all this that I had behaved like a kid, but I was very happy. So happy. I got the cherished photograph back.

"Oh, that is why you did not come yesterday for the opening day of my school ! You won't believe me but I was kind of waiting for you to come," I said.

"Yes. I thought it better not to bother you for a day," he said giving a laugh, which by now, I had embedded in my memory. It didn't any longer irritate or annoy me. It felt comforting now.

"Not at all. Hey you want tea or coffee?" I said.

"Come. Let's brew it together. Green tea is fine for me," he said.

While sipping tea, I shared that I was leaving for Kolkata the same afternoon. His expression changed and he looked disturbed.

"But I thought you were here for a few more days. You never shared your plans before." He began to frown.

And why was I supposed to announce my plans or changes in them to him. I wondered.

"Yes, that was the plan earlier, but I have to go today. I have some legal documents to sort out – some final official papers I have to sign for my NGO." I sighed and said.

"Legal formalities. Oh then I can't stop you from going. But I have a question which rings in my mind non-stop. How can he leave you?" he said this while looking deep into my eyes.

"We left each other. It was a mutual decision," I said.

"How can anyone leave you – whatsoever the reason may be?" His gaze was so intense now that it was making me quite uncomfortable and uneasy. I wanted to walk away.

"What? It was a mutual decision. We decided to, so we left each other. That's it!" The nervous note in my voice broke his steady gaze.

"Well Noya, the fact is that I'm just not prepared to say goodbye to you. I went to Delhi thinking I had today and many more days to discuss our professional partnership. If I had known earlier that you were leaving today, I would have postponed my Delhi plans," he said.

But why would you postpone your business meetings for meeting me, Ranbir? My mind started shooting questions. But I dare not ask him.

"Don't worry. We can still do it over the phone. And it was for the better that you went to Delhi. See, I have my wallet back with me!" I said, smiling.

"But I can't see your expressions over the phone. I love seeing your unpredictable and spontaneous asseverations. You know, there is so much I want to hear from you. I want to know you. I want to know what you eat, what you like, when you feel happy, when you don't, when you are scared, when you are sad, what you do when you are hungry, what you do when you are sleepy, what you do when you are with family, with your friends, with your pets, what you watch on TV, how you reply to your messages, how you post on your social network..." he said gazing at me as he went on breathlessly, effortlessly.

"Why? Am I some sort of a practical research topic which you can experiment in your laboratory?" I asked. "Bye Ranbir. Hope to see you soon. Okay, I have to go now and get ready or else I will miss my flight," I said.

"Bye for now. We will meet very soon," he said.

"I will call you from there and we can catch up. I'm late already!" I said looking at the timepiece put up on the wall.

"Alright Noya. And before you leave, I have got something for you." He said while taking out a wrapped square shaped gift.

"I don't like taking gifts from anyone." I snapped.

"But I have got this for you. I won't like it if you don't take it."

"Alright. I will take it. For you. But don't bring it again."

Before the flight took off, I remembered the gift he had presented me and took it out from my handbag. I opened the wrapper which had glittering red stars on the base of shiny glossy silver paper. The gift was a watch and there was a small note inside the box saying – 'Times have changed. You have to fly high. You deserve all the happiness. I hope whenever you wear the watch, you remember there is a friend in this world who wants you to be yourself. Not this camouflaged Noya. But the real Noya, who you have hidden somewhere deep inside you. And to get back to the real you, you have to forego all that had happened and look forward to your present and the future. Shed all fear, forget all worries, be immune to criticism and be fearless. For life is one and you can't be living like you are, just because something unpleasant has happened. Now smile. You look beautiful and confident when you smile.'

I interpreted that he wants me to forget my past and focus on the future and live life happily. I took out the gift from the box and wore it. It was my friendship band. I smiled.

I texted to thank him for the considerate gift and message. But before I could receive any reply, the air hostess announced the takeoff and I had to switch off the phone half-heartedly.

On reaching Kolkata, I directly went to the court and completed the document work. While getting inside the car, I saw a little bird perched on the roof. I talked with it before driving away -

"I'm free... like you are!" I shouted at the hovering bird above me. "I love you birdie... I love you. Fly high... live your life."

My cell beeped. There were three messages from Ranbir. *'Glad you liked the gift. And I hope next time we meet, I see more smiles and less frowns.'*

'Hi, how are you? I didn't hear from you. Thought you would at least inform me that you had reached.'

'I'm planning to open a branch of my jewellery chain 'BM- Bling Me' in Kolkata. Care to be the manager? You stay in Kolkata so you can take care of things in there.'

My surging fingers and heart fought with my reluctant and restrictive mind over whether or not to reply to his messages.

But finally I did.

'Ranbir, I was always an average academic student. I scored in the eighties till the tenth. After that, I always just managed to get into the first division. I was always more inclined towards and interested in extra-curricular activities – social work, animal welfare, literary activities, dance. What contribution can I make to your company? It's better if you appoint a good manager. I working for you would mean disaster,' I replied. I texted that way just for the sake of it. I knew that in reality, only scores don't depict whether you can be a good or a bad manager. Your skills matter too.

I kept checking my phone for a reply, but long hours passed and there were none from him.

Two days passed. Still no trace of him. It was a tug of war inside me – a part of me wanting to avoid him, while the other part wanting to know why he hadn't responded. However little I knew of him, I knew that he was not the sort who wouldn't follow up with me.

My mixed feelings tempted me to send him a text to enquire if he was well. The previous night I had thought of all sorts of reasons why he hadn't replied.

Maybe he wanted to finally get rid of me and my babbling…

Maybe he thought I was too dumb to contribute to his company in any way…

Or maybe he had met with an accident and was lying in the ICU with his eyes closed, without any access to a communication device. Did his family know that he was in the hospital? I hoped someone was near him, tending to him, caring for him…

I trembled at the last thought and prayed that nothing had happened to him.

Sometimes in life you meet vivacious people who touch your heart. You never get to know much about these people, but you like it when they are around you, even when they don't speak a word to you. Their presence makes the ambience exciting and worthwhile. For me, he had become one such person. I didn't want to talk to him or know about him, but I did enjoy his presence. I liked it when he was around. The feeling was similar to that unspoken and unsurpassable feeling you get when you are inside a confectionary, chocolate, toy or a book store.

Unable to restrain myself, I sent him a text at night, just before I was about to hit my bed.

'Is everything fine? How are you?'

No reply.

In the morning, the first thing I did was rush to Dad and ask him for the contact number of Aryan Mallya, from whom I could take Ranbir's landline number. I didn't know, neither did I want to understand why was I behaving so desperately, but I just knew that I had to get in touch with him. My frightening thoughts had percolated through my mind, my heart and were piercing my soul.

Mr Aryan Mallya's secretary gave me the prized contact number.

Ting. Ting. Ting. Ting. I pressed the buttons on my cellphone and waited nervously.

A male voice answered the call.

But it was not his.

I disconnected the call in an instant. I had not prepared any excuse for the call. I was still thinking about this when the same landline number flashed on my screen. Whoever it was, was calling back. My heart skipped several beats when I answered and heard the much awaited voice. I in a flash felt peaceful, as if all the pressure inside me was easing.

"Noya, what happened? Why did you cut the call? It was my cousin that time. Now tell me what happened. It's me now," he said.

"How are you? I was worried for you so I thought of calling. I thought you would respond to my texts but you did not. I know you are not the type to not respond to someone's texts," I began feebly.

"Does it really matter to you?" he asked.

"Yes," I paused. "It does." What was I saying! "A bit." I added to play it safe. I was just scared to plunge into any kind of new relationships.

"You don't find contact numbers with such effort and call up people to ask how they are, for a bit of care, do you? You never even pegged me as a friend. In the beginning, I was helping you as a human being, but gradually I started genuinely caring and liking you as a friend. But you never reciprocated. Whenever I tried coming closer to you, you made me feel like some kind of a stalking pervert. For you, I'm still a stalker and some bloody, gluey prospect who wants to marry you. But all that I wanted was to be a friend to you. I have seen you from the day you boarded the train at Howrah till the day you left for Kolkata. You are such a confident, determined and courageous girl deep inside, but for some reason you have hidden that to display a pretentious facet. Just because you went through a painful ordeal doesn't mean you forget yourself, your life, your happiness. You have just halted your life. You are scared to even befriend me. Your insecurities are making you stay away from people who care for you. All men are not like your ex-boyfriend. I don't know what the problems between you and him were. But all that I want to say is to respect yourself, move on, find meaning in your life and live happily. You look lovely when you smile." I was amazed how he managed to talk so breathlessly and yet sound so sensible.

And he paused till he restarted -

"And I want to share another news. Tomorrow, we have an engagement function at my house. She is the daughter of one of my mom's friends. I wanted to invite you, but I felt it would hurt you if you saw another engagement after your recent break-up and all that has happened, so I didn't. Please, just take good care of yourself. And know it, I'm always there for you. Leave your ego and do contact me whenever you feel like it. Ok, Noya, I got to go. Mom is calling me. Got to go shopping. This marriage has been a hurried decision so we have a lot of planning and shopping to do."

"That's great news. Bye." After that long oration, those were the only words I uttered. I was comatose. Ranbir getting engaged! I couldn't believe what I had just heard. Isn't he too young to get married? But didn't I plan to get married when I was twenty-four!

"Always say bye for now. I don't like byes." He said.

'Congratulations Ranbir!' I texted later.

'Aren't you opening the branch here in Kolkata?' The second message followed.

Once again, there was no reply.

That night, I couldn't sleep till 3.00 a.m. and merely tossed in bed. Finally, I got up and stood in front of the mirror. After a long look, I repeated his discourse to myself. His words made sense. We have one life – one short life. Why was I holding myself back for some insensitive person who didn't have enough guts and love inside him to survive the relationship? It wasn't my fault. I took his photographs from the locker of my wardrobe and, shedding tears, went to the balcony, lit a candle and burnt them all. Soon a small flame raged and fumes blew all around.

After a minute, the fire alarms blew up and an automated voice shrieked:

> *"There is an emergency, I request all of the house members to rush to the garden assembly point."*
>
> *"Second Reminder. There is an emergency, I request all of the house members to rush to the garden assembly point. Please hurry."*
>
> *"Third Reminder. I request all of the house members to rush to the garden assembly point. Room 1 all clear, Room 2 all clear, Room 3 all clear... Kitchen all clear, Room 4 balcony one person. Rush to the garden assembly point immediately. This is*

an alert that in Room 4 balcony, one person is stuck, his path to the nearest emergency exit is clear. Please run to the garden through emergency exit no. 4."

Oh, what I have done! I ran to the garden where my parents, pets, servers, housekeepers and drivers were assembled.

"Fourth Reminder. I request all of the house members to assemble at the garden assembly point. Please rush. House is all clear. Source of flame identified. Room no. 4, balcony. Nearest fire brigade alerted. It will reach in another minute. It is on the way."

Oh God. Weren't there enough problems in life that this embarrassment had to unfold?

Meekly, like a mouse would in front of a cat, I spoke, "Mom and Dad, I'm sorry but there's nothing to worry about. I was exiting a person out of my life and so the alarm buzzed up."

"Darling, it is such a sensible decision to shoo a person's memory away. Please don't apologize to us. Now, since we have already gathered here on the lawns…Girish! Light up the fire wood and switch on the barbeque. Let's party!" Dad said smiling.

My mother embraced me in a hug. Not a moment in life had she ever made me feel that she was a step-mother. My own mother, Kavya, had succumbed to cancer when I was three years and all that I remembered about her was her face in the photo I carried with me always. And the message she had written for me –

'Noya, my darling daughter. Always know that you are not alone. My prayers and blessings are always with you. Make sure your father remarries as he is not the type to manage it alone on

the home front. And I'm always there. Every time you miss me, just see my face in this photograph. See the stars in the sky. I will be one of those, looking at you, smiling at you. All my life, I stood honest and brave. I want my daughter to be courageous. Don't let the world defeat you at any point of time. When you think you can, you will. Always be happy my child. I love you.'

Kavya Agnihotri

"I love you guys. You are my world." I hugged my parents. "And you are the best daughter in the world!" they chorused.

Buzz...buzzzzzzz...buzzzzzzzzzz...buzzzzzzzzzz

I woke with to the vibrating phone at 11.00 a.m. It was a call from Rohan.

Sheepishly, I answered. "Hi Rohan, what happened? Tell me quickly. I slept at 6.00 a.m. yesterday...oops I mean today. And so I need to sleep," I somehow managed to put together a coherent sentence.

"Oh, alright. Are you drunk?" he asked.

"Shut up. You know I'm a teetotaller if you ignore that one day, and tell me what it is. I will give you the details later when we meet," I said almost sounding as if I'm declaring myself to be a virgin.

"Okay, we are planning a trip to Goa. Are you in?"

"We?" I asked.

"Rima, Ayan, Gourav, Kriti," he replied.

"No, you guys go. I have some important work here," I said.

"Don't say that. Try, please. It won't be fun without the entire group," he said with persistence.

"No, I won't be able to. I'm sorry," I said.

"You are sleepy. Wake up and give me a buzz in case you change your mind. In the meantime, I will tell Rima and Kriti that you are not coming. They will definitely convince you, so I'm going to book your tickets anyway," he said.

"No, don't book my tickets as I won't be able to come," I said and dropped the call.

I put my head under the pillow to get away from the world and closed my eyes, only to open them a moment later. Did he say Goa?

"They have planned a trip to Goa!" I screamed to myself.

'Rohan, count me in. I have some unfinished business in Goa,' I texted him later.

'I have already booked your tickets. I was damn sure you would be joining.' He replied.

'☺ *Can't thank you enough for that'*.

It was payback time. I needed to extend my friendship to someone who deserved it. My inappropriate and insensitive behaviour towards him had been giving me sleepless nights and I had to regain my peace.

"Here I come, Goa. Here I come, Ranbir!"

When the flight landed at Dabolim Airport, my heart was racing like a Formula One Ferrari. I had come without any concrete plans. I had no idea what I'd do next, what I would say to Ranbir, how I would apologize or even where I would meet him.

And to add to it all, his relationship status was no longer single. It was all so awkward. When he had been trying to be friendly, I had behaved like a maniac, and now that he was engaged, I had flown all the way from the east to the south west of India. It is well said that the worth of true relationships is felt when the person is out of sight, yet constantly in mind. It is amazing what a person who is miles away can do to you. Such people do exist in the world who make an impact in your life.

I started planning a series of conversations that could encapsulate what I would say to Ranbir and oh, his fiancée. I assumed his fiancée would be as well behaved, polite and sensitive as Ranbir – after all, birds of a feather flock together. But then, that isn't true in most relationships. Opposites attract often.

"Hello Fiancée." *I didn't know her name and had not bothered to ask Ranbir either.* "I'm Ranbir's self-proclaimed good friend, who has never behaved well with him. For all the good he has done to me, I feel this is the best time to do some good for him. That's why I planned this trip to meet both of you like a good girl."

Gosh, that sounded like an English grammar lesson – completely antiquated.

After a few more lame rehearsals, I decided I would say what my heart and mind felt impromptu when I met him or her or both of them.

Ting. Ting. Ting. Ting.

I dialled Ranbir's landline number from a public phone booth to maintain a degree of anonymity. Why I had resorted to this, I didn't know. I was just behaving on the go.

I planned to find out whether he was in Goa, then to summon him to some place by giving a fake identity and then surprising him with the fact that it had been me all along.

"Hello."

My thoughts were interrupted by a sweet, accented voice.

I disconnected the call and came out of the booth. I went inside again and dialled the number, steeling myself to the idea that no matter who attended my call, I would ask for Ranbir and speak to him directly.

"Hello…Hello…Hello…can you say something please?" the same woman asked. Why was I not saying anything? I had never been such a meek person. What had happened to me? Was it some nervous breakdown disease I had contracted?

I meticulously tried for the third time, this time almost assuring myself that I would speak. Also, there was a queue of three people standing behind me to use the phone. So I had to be successful this time.

The dame picked up the phone after the numero uno ring. Was she sitting there awaiting the call from an unknown, dumb person? Whatever, such a call does intrigue one.

Before she could speak, I said, "Hello, is Ranbir there? I'm his school friend, Ritwika."

"Yeah, sure. Ranbir baby, it's for you. Hey, be careful! Don't drop the engagement ring!"

Who is calling Ranbir a baby – what was happening? Who was she? I thought and imagined Ranbir with this sexy woman in his room, on his bed, on his couch, on him.

"Hello. This is Ranbir on the line. Finally I heard that soothing voice for which I had come all the way.

"Ranbir, this is Ritwika from school. I'm in Goa for work and have some business with you. Can you meet me at the Taj today at 6.00 p.m.?" I attempted to make my voice gruff.

"Ritwika? Sorry, but I can't recollect that I know anyone named Ritika, from school, college or business. I think you have dialled a wrong number," he said and hung up.

Before hanging up, I overheard him telling to the girl – "I guess my friend is again playing the same prank. Just ignore it."

Oops. Couldn't I have chosen some other common name? What could I do next? I went back to the house where my friends and I were putting up.

Rima, Ayan, Gourav, Kriti and Rohan were ready and waiting for me to go to Anjuna beach. When we reached, the girls planned to visit the flea market. The guys went to reserve a shack and start boozing.

In the flea market, name any commodity or piece of apparel and you have it – in various shapes, colours and prices. It's heaven for a shopaholic.

Deeply engrossed in shopping, we paid no attention to where we were going and so lost our way. We asked the nearby shopkeepers for the way out and followed their directions, but we still reached the wrong place. Confused, we stood there and again asked a few people for directions to reach the shack. It was in some place called Hoppers' Hop. Seeing our plight, a girl in her twenties came up to us on a bike.

"Hop on," she said.

"What?" we looked at each other.

"Come on. Sit on my bike. I will drop you," she said.

"But we can walk. Can you just guide us with the directions? We need to reach Hoppers' Hop," I said.

She parked the bike, came up to us and whispered in our ears. "See, it is evening now. And you have lost your way. This lane is dangerous. It's where you will find all the drug addicts, thugs and thieves. So just come with me."

Thanks to our skinny frames, we all managed to fit on the bike.

Soon, we reached the place where the boys were playing beach volleyball with a few other tourists.

"Hey, hey, Ayan!" Rimi shouted, getting off the bike. Ayan threw the ball to another guy and ran over to us.

"Where were you all? It's been four hours!" he said.

"You were playing beach volleyball. We were playing lane hopping," I said, winking at the new girl. "Anyways, this is..." Oops. I had not asked her name.

"Jenny," she said.

"Thanks for your help Jenny," I said.

"Any time," she said.

"How did you girls fit onto this bike? And how come a girl is riding a bike.. she is strong and fit for sure...and Oh man, is this a Harley Davidson? Are you filthy rich or a member of the famed drug mafia group?" Ayan asked Jenny jokingly.

"Ayan. Stop bothering her," Rima pitched in.

"Dear Ayan, I'm the girlfriend of Don Booka Looka. Have you heard of him? The most wanted criminal. Anything else you want to know about me or my boyfriend?" Jenny winked at us.

I got the catch here. To pacify Ayan, who looked shocked. I said, "Ayan, if you ask dangerous questions, you will obviously get scary answers. We got lost in a dark lane and she was our saviour. She offered us a ride here."

"Oh, I see. We always give a treat to those who help us. So, Miss Booka Looka, care to join us for a party at Britto's tonight?" Ayan asked looking and winking at Rima to persuade and invite Jenny.

We stood there shocked. Ayan was not the kind of guy who hit on other hot and pretty girls he came across. He was more the brotherly kind, who was there for any girl in need. He was the types who was friend-zoned - the goody goody boy.

"Jenny, please join us. We would really like it," Rima said.

Finally, Jenny agreed. "I already had a party lined up, so do you mind if I invite four other friends?"

"As long as they are not Booka Looka's men, we are fine with it," Ayan said.

"Done, guys. See you at eight thirty," Jenny said and left.

The other guys could not stop laughing and taunting Ayan when they heard about the episode from Kriti. They looked forward to the party to get to know some new people.

"Hello guys, this is Drishti, Samveda, Cora, Gourav…and here she comes, our girl of the evening, Meera."

I turned my head to see a gorgeous girl entering the shack and greeting, "Hi, Jenny". Her height made even the boys look shorter. Her impeccable perfect looks made every head turn towards her. I thought in my mind that if I ever get close to this girl, I would take make-up training classes from her.

"Hey Meera. So glad you could make it tonight. Love you, babes." Jenny and the girl hugged, pecked each other on the cheeks.

Meera was a hot and charming girl. She was tall, with big, bright, beautiful eyes, wavy hair and a slim and fair body, but when she opened her mouth, all that came out were swear words. Her persona and behaviour didn't quite match. Whatever, I ignored it all. I was there only for the party. I was not interested in any tips from her. I preferred the internet now. She was also quite insensitive towards the servers. That was when I had to pitch in and asked her to tone down a bit as she was sounding really rude. I didn't think it went down with her well, as after that, she kind of avoided interacting with me. And every time someone from her group talked with me, she intentionally interrupted the conversation. I chose to avoid her as well. Next day she would be elsewhere and I will be another place. Why bother!

Around the round table, Ayan sat between Jenny and Meera. I saw Ayan looking at both in turns as though deciding who was better of the two.

Trying to be polite and warm, he complimented Meera's dress.

"Are you complimenting the dress or the sizzling body inside this dress?" Meera said.

Her response made Ayan turn his chair and head towards Jenny. Now it seemed he was sure who the better of the two was. Ayan dilated his eyes and looked at me. His eyes asked, "Who is she?"

Jenny pulled me up to dance. While everyone else danced in a boy-girl pair, Jenny and I danced in a girl-girl pair. Ayan signalled to me to come back to the table and allow him to dance with Jenny.

Soon everyone was on the round dance floor except for me, Kriti, Rima and Cora. Red, yellow and green lights from the ceiling flashed on the floor. The dance floor was also set with glittering and shimmering lights. Everyone except me was getting intoxicated by the booze. I chose not to drink any strong spirit today. I tried red wine this time. I sat on the chair performing the role of a dedicated nanny, looking after all their purses and valuables.

Jenny and Ayan; Meera and Rohan; Samveda and some stranger; Drishti and Gourav; the couples swayed to the beat of the thumping music.

"Hey Cora, don't you like to dance?" Rima tried to break the ice between us.

"I do, but not with this group. I came just for Drishti's sake. I don't hang out much with others . And the other girl is such a harsh-hearted girl."

Rima, being the curious sort, tried to pry out more information through her social skills. "And why would you say that? She seems to be such a cool and cute girl."

I knew that Rima was digging for information. I had already seen her pulling a face at things Meera had said that evening.

"Cool girl! God save her. Even the devil will shy away when he meets her. You know she is getting married to some rich guy? God only knows how she will lead a married life. All she has done till now was to hop from one guy to another. Don't tell anyone this, but she has not broken up with her long distance boyfriend yet and has made marriage plans with him too. She said that she will tell him the news of her engagement after her birthday. It seems he has planned some vacation in Kerala and has promised her a diamond ring and an expensive car. So she has plans to take it all, then dump him and then marry a richer person. Her life has always been a materialistic one – running in front of and behind the rich brats. Her name suggests she is a well-cultured girl, but she is just the opposite. There was one Meera Bai who was an ardent worshipper and lover of Lord Krishna. And here in this century, there is this Meera – ardent follower of rich guys and their bank accounts." Cora blurted all this out under the influence of the red wine she had been drinking.

"Oh, here they come. Shh!" I said to Cora, tapping the table to alert her. I saw the dancers returning like the wave of an ocean, flowing from the dance floor to the tables.

The next day, I decided I would end this game of hide and seek that I seemed to be playing. I would call Ranbir and tell him I am in town and wanted to meet him. So I excused myself from my friends on the pretext of going to my school. I told them I would join them later. They were going to Meera's house as she had invited them over. The plan was to spend the whole day touring Goa on bikes and indulge in some water sports, and then to stay the night at Meera's. For some reason, I didn't want to join them in the night either but I had to move with the tide. I was also scared to spend the night alone in the huge bungalow. Samaira too was out of station so my second option was ruled out. My third option was checking into a hotel. I preferred the last one.

I went to Eme and spent time with the children and had lunch with them. I had ordered pizza from a food chain – a special treat from me for the children who were working hard to become earning members of their families. After lunch, I went to the church to pray. As I lit a candle, I saw another hand beside mine, also lighting a candle. It had a familiar platinum ring on the thumb. My heart skipped some beats. My knees felt weak. My breath speeded. I turned to the look at the face.

"Ranbir, what are you doing here?" I asked, flabbergasted at the concurrence of events.

"Noya, what a pleasant surprise! Pinch me. Is it really you? Couldn't you give me a ring or send me a text telling me you are here?" he said.

How could I tell him how many times I had tried to reach him, or that I had planned surprise meetings? It had all been in vain.

"Okay, listen, I have been busy so I could not text or call you. I have been trying to find some time for you." I said. My ego was taking over again.

"Whatever Noya, let's not mess up this amazing coincidence," he said, his smile big and wide now.

"Hey, so are you engaged now? Show me your engagement ring," I said.

"Not yet. She had to go abroad on important work so we had to postpone the engagement. We've set dates for next month. And this time, you have to come," he said.

"Will I be invited this time?" I asked.

"Why not?" he said.

"Ok Ranbir. Before my mind again takes over my thoughts, I need to say this. I mean I have never given you a place in my life. But now I'm asking for some. I want to be your good friend – will you accept me as your good friend?" I asked.

"Oh, you are so kiddish. And that is what I love about you. You are just so different from the others. So naïve. So true. Anyway, thanks. I'm so privileged to be your good friend," Ranbir said, stretching the 'good'. "Oh Noya, I missed you so much. I don't know whether you missed me or not," he said.

"Isn't it too early to miss someone? And we haven't actually mingled or interacted much, so I didn't," I said. Though inside my heart I knew, I had been kind of yearning for his presence in my life all these days.

"First of all, clear my query on your spiritual trip. Why were you on that trip? I'm dying of curiosity at the perfect concurrent meetings of ours all this while," I asked.

"Oh that trip! It was not to be after you, but for my father. He was hospitalised due to a stroke. It was then that I had prayed for him and decided to go on a spiritual trip to Haji Ali, the Golden Temple, the Jagannath Temple, Rameswaram, Vaishno Devi, and St Thomas Church. Now you understand why I was on that tour. It was not to stalk you," he said while and closing his eyes for a minute to pray.

"Hey let's go to my house. Mom and Dad will be happy to meet you. I have told them so much about you," he said after opening his eyes.

"Not today, some other day please. Look at me. I don't want to go to your home for the very first time in shorts," I said while winking at him. "Tell me about your girlfriend."

"She is not my girlfriend," he said while looking away.

"How did you meet her?" I asked. I wanted to know more.

"You want to talk the universe here. Let's go to Eme. We will meet the kids and also chitchat."

As I sip coffee in the office room, I hear him out. "She is the daughter of one of my mom's friends. When we were kids, Mom had casually promised this friend that she would make me marry her daughter."

"Pheeeeeee...."

I squeaked before I erupted into laughter. "How can you marry someone for this reason? Because your mother promised her friend? I have seen these things in century-old movies. Do you love her?" I asked.

"Love...no. In fact, I'm not even attached to her yet, emotionally. My feelings are just in the native stage, you know, that formative period of love," he said.

His use of the word 'formative' made me think of the gestation period of a baby. When it's forming, it's inside your body and when it's fully grown, it emerges from within you. Love is similar.

"Hmm. So what's her name?" I asked.

"Niti," he said.

"Wow, nice name. It sounds like that of a perfect, suave, goody girlfriend who will become a very good wife," I said.

"She is almost perfect. See, one day I have to get married. I was reluctant to marry in the beginning, but when I saw Niti, I found her so well behaved and suited to my personality and traits, so I thought, why not marry her? I know it's still in a premature stage, but I'm really trying to develop love for her," he said.

"How long have you known each other?" I asked.

"A month," he said. Something in his eyes was saying he was least interested in the girl. Or was it my pangs of jealousy. Ranbir can't have another girl in his life. Am I not the one who was the most important for him? At least his actions spoke so.

"And you are trying to get some love for her. Love is not a commodity that you can buy and use," I said.

"Jesus, is this the same Noya who I have been meeting? Look, she is talking so sensibly now! I have never heard you blabber so much," he said.

"Am I blabbering? I'm talking sense!" I said. "I have always respected you in my heart, thinking of you as a confident, determined and courageous man. You remember that long speech you gave me on the day I called you, that was the game changer in my life. That was the moment I told myself – no more. No more tears for those who don't deserve them, no more lacunae in my life for some cold ruthless boyfriend who is non-existent for me now," I said this and tears just rolled down from my eyes.

"A year from now, the things which are stressing you won't even matter. So is it worth to spoil your present moments. Grow up Noya," he said

"I know I shouldn't look back. But it's as if I'm still chained to my past. I'm also a human being. I have a mind. I have a heart. Wouldn't it pain if the person turns out to be completely opposite to what you had expected. How could he have been so materialistic, cold and insensitive." I said and broke down.

"I want to know more about you. I really do. I don't want to know about your past for curiosity's sake. I feel I should know about you as now I'm a good friend of yours. And good friends should know about each other. Come on, let's go to the beach. Let us sit there and talk. Talking it out will release the pain inside you," he said.

We sat at one of the short bamboo tables topped by red cloth, on wooden chairs.

As I sipped on my sparkling wine, I began my story. He sat listening to me intently, sipping his single malt drink, all ears.

"It was the orientation day in my college. That was when I saw him for the first time. All the first year students had been summoned to the college auditorium. He wouldn't have caught my attention if he hadn't been in those bright green trousers and red shirt – he looked like an advertisement for a beach tour. Out of all the blue, grey, brown, purple, pale green, it was the outstanding bright green pants with the white belt that stood out. To add to that, he was wearing yellow floaters and a red and black checked shirt with dog tags out of the gap left by the one open button of the shirt. He was definitely the head turner of the day. Even the guys were ignoring the prettiest damsels and turning their heads towards him.

He was seated in the same row as mine, the fourth row. The first row was meant for the supposed special dignitaries – the owners, sponsors, guests, dean, senior professors and some senior students. The second and third were occupied by the other professors and students. The arriving students had to sit as they came. It was first come, first take. The seniors didn't leave us with an option to sit wherever we liked. That is when I got introduced to Priyanka who sat to my left. I got to know then that we both were day boarders. The induction function was followed by some inspirational speeches from the guests.

❖

When we saw him entering our classroom, his choice of colour compatibility seemed to indicate he should have instead chosen a course of Fashion Technology and reinvented his taste and palate, but there he was, sitting in the commerce section. Oh God, why was he approaching me? Soon, he took the seat right next to mine. That concluded he belonged to my section and course.

Priyanka, sitting on my left, looked at me and nudged me with her elbow. She smiled at me and whispered, "Enjoy, babe. The class looks so delightfully colourful and interesting now."

"Good morning, students. I see bright minds, faces and clothes," said the professor while entering. She looked at the boy sitting next to me when she said 'clothes'.

I realized that if I sat next to him, I would definitely be in the spotlight of the professors and other students and I didn't want that. I had to text and chit chat during the classes and it would be impossible if fancy colours caught the attention of everyone else. So I said to Priyanka, "I want us to move back. Any ideas?"

"Cough like you have a frog in the throat and go out of the class. Tell the professor you are dizzy. I will feign that I will have to accompany you home and so we can bunk and catch a movie. Salman's blockbuster has released today and we are wasting time in the classroom," she suggested.

"But I want to attend the class," I said.

"Throw water. The floor, table and chair will get soppy, and we can move back," she said.

"But it will also result in this guy moving back with us. This is against our best interests," I said in conflict.

"But that's the best act we can do with the available resources," she said.

I opened my water bottle and brought it to my lips. I blew hard and threw the water on the desk.

"Oh baba!" Priyanka screamed and raised her hand.

"What happened there, Priyanka Gulati?" asked the professor annoyed with the commotion caused in the middle of his serious explanation of a complex graph explaining country's GDP growth over the years.

"Ma'am, we spilled water on our tables and chairs. We will have to move back," said Priyanka.

"Alright, but quickly. You people are disturbing the entire class."

Disturbing the entire class! Did she have any idea what the students in the last rows were doing? Circulating chits, texting, watching movies, talking on the phone with heads bowed down. Some were even snoring.

Sitting at the back, I took a quick look at the yellow shirt and blue pants guy. His head had his spiky hair standing up, glued together with hair setting gel. Who on earth had ever told him that his sense of styling was good?

"Noya, what is an Aggressive growth fund?" My glance was interrupted.

I stood up after typing 'aggressive growth fund' on the internet browser of my mobile.

Round and round it rotated but the speed was just too imperceptible.

"You can sit and answer. We are no longer in school," she said crabbily.

I looked at my mobile but in vain. "A growth fund which is aggressive…and furious and which is available to the public easily. Which tempts people immediately to invest in. Is that it?" I asked.

"Nonsense. No wonder I saw you looking at the blank wall. Pay attention in class else I fear for your results," warned the professor.

"Oh God! What was I blabbering?" I said dejected.

Priyanka tried cheering me up as we walked to the statistics lab. We tried to sit together but the ruthless professor said, "Priyanka, go to Table 4 and Noya goes to 10."

Priyanka now sat opposite me with the hottest guy in the class. They were conversing more than doing any work on the trend graphs. I sat with the bright Prakrit who was working on the case put forth by the professor. He did the actual work while I sat texting.

"Ma'am, we did it," he said.

'We?' I had not even touched it.

"Did you both do it or just you?" the professor asked.

"We both did it," he said, giving me a quick glance.

During the ten minute break between classes, he asked me to have a cup of coffee with him. I had to agree out of gratitude. After all, the first impression lasts a long time and he had helped me make a good one on the lab professor.

While sipping caffeine in the canteen, we didn't know what to talk about and so we ended up speaking zilch. Just exchanged meaningless smiles with each other. We just didn't have anything in common. I pretended to be busy fiddling with my cell. I also kept looking at the time on my phone and the canteen clock. Ten minutes went by very slowly; a tortoise would have walked faster. I was relieved when we walked back to class.

He sat next to me in the next class and the following days. Priyanka had a new time pass - of teasing and taunting every time I looked at her or him.

After a week, miraculously as if God heard, I swapped with another girl and got different lab mates and so I could honestly avoid Mr Bright for a valid reason. In the classroom too, the professor allotted us specific seats so I got spared from sitting with him. One year passed and we were nothing more than batch-mates, exchanging just a muttered 'Hi' whenever we encountered each other. Though his words were few, his gazes were always prolonged. Every time I felt his eyes were on me, it made me feel queasy.

And then one fine day, Tathagat – the placement officer – barged into the ongoing class and called out mine, Priyanka and Prakrit's names.

"What have we done?" Priyanka mimed to me.

"Oh, have we been caught bunking that macro economics class?" I said.

"Or is it that warning I gave to the boy from Science section who kept roses on my bench?" she said.

I hinted at her with narrowed eyes, to wait and see before arriving to any conclusions.

"Follow me." We trailed him to the Dean's office.

We were relieved when we saw the Dean smile – we had not committed any nuisance after all. There were another fourteen to sixteen students standing inside the dainty and decorated office. It was bedecked with awards and accolades, certificates, gifts and mementos and hmmm…a *Cosmopolitan* magazine on his table. Not that I was expecting *Playboy*. We saw him quickly sneaking it into his drawer after he realized all our eyes on the cover page – a model clad in bikini with her waist bent down and a considerable part of her dusky cleavage at show. The sea in the backdrop made her look hotter.

"Hello students! You must be wondering why I have summoned you. We have been invited to a cultural fest in Mumbai at Jehangir College. It's supposedly the biggest cultural fest in India, with participants coming from colleges across the country. We have selected you all based on educational background, references, recommendations and interests. Participate in it. We wish you all the best. Tathagat will mail you further details of the programme," he said.

"And now we officially have the prestigious licence to bunk humdrum pernicious classes and practice for our fest. Yahoo!" Priyanka shouted just after exiting the Dean's office.

"Priya, I know, you have started writing these blogs and stuff, but keep the difficult words restricted to that! Those are not for normal conversation, dear. I mean sticking to a dictionary is fine when I'm reading a book. Do you expect me to carry one while talking to you too? No way, honey."

"Oh yeah. In short what I mean is shitty classes."

"Come on, classes are never crap. It's we students who make it seem like that," I said.

"Oh. Here you go again! I will make a note of it. Sorry. Ooh I'm so excited. I love you, Dean. I love you." Just as she said it, the Dean came to the door of his room, where we were standing.

We both stood like statues, unsure what to say at the unexpected sight of his, after Priya blurting out those awkward words.

"Sorry, sir. I was too excited about the fest and was thanking you from the bottom of my heart," Priyanka said.

"It's all right. But do not behave like this again. Lucky for you that only I heard it. If my wife had, I would be in a sorry state now."

Saying this, he winked at us and walked away.

"Oh look at that. Our seemingly strict Dean cracks jokes. These days, people have multiple personalities – one for the world, one for the family, one for friends and one for oneself. Let's go to the classroom, get our bags and start our preparations right away," said Priyanka.

"But where is Prakrit?" I asked.

"He must have joined some other team. Forget him," she said.

When we entered the cultural hall, we found it already packed with the groups practicing – some dancing, some acting out a skit, and some a silent play.

"Hey, see, Prakrit is dancing with the boys of another Commerce batch. Didn't I tell you that he must have paired up with someone else," said Priyanka, pointing at the boys dancing to hip hop music.

We ignored him and joined the girls of the Humanities section. I sat down behind the drums, Priyanka and Namrata tested the mike to check if their melodious voices were audible and Maya took to the keyboard. We practiced a song composed by Priyanka. It was one of the songs she had written during her high school days.

While I was drumming in sync with the singing duo and the keyboard, I saw Prakrit approaching me.

"Hey girls, can you practice after we finish? You see, we came here before you and your *'dhoom dhoom dhan dhan'* is distracting our concentration. We are unable to hear our music. So will you please bear with us and help us out?"

"How rude," Priyanka's expression seemed to say. She didn't utter a word while packing her bag and helping us do the same.

We called Rehan, Namrata's school friend who owned a music studio, and booked it for practice sessions in the evening hours. He was kind enough to agree to our request and resolve our problem.

After this, we avoided Prakrit completely and Priyanka made sure that I never even exchanged the usual greetings or smiles with him.

Mumbai – the land of the placid sea, warm people and endless night life. This is a place where everyone dwells together in sanctity and at peace with one another. All festivals are celebrated in harmony – a perfect example of unity in diversity. The city is not partial to anyone and has a bounty of love and opportunities for its entire people.

Prakrit's hip hop team won the runners up prize at the fest. We won the first place in the 'innovative fusion' category as we had presented an indo-fusion song.

We soon became the famous five and performed in college functions thereafter.

Our college days rolled by very fast like a dice in a game and soon it was the final month of our course. The entire batch planned a trip. Considering the scorching heat of the blazing bright sun, we planned an expedition to Ooty – queen of the hills.

I love hill stations as they are pristine and rejuvenating. We checked into the Youth Hostel and rushed to occupy the best beds near the electrical sockets, to charge our best friends – our electronic gadgets. But oh! There was not a single damn socket in this long rectangular dorm! Only twenty beds lined up next to each other in a neat row. I heard some friends shrieking in the washroom as if they had found some treasure. I rushed there only to find them pushing each other to reach the hallowed power socket.

Ting. Ting.

My battery was giving a few beeps before dying out. I had to do something. It struck me that I could ask the boys if they had had any better luck. I believe that luck is abundant in the world. It's just that if one is unlucky in one case, it means God has given that share of luck to someone else.

I looked here and there, running out from the girl's dorm to the reception. There was a socket there. I befriended the receptionist and used the situation to my benefit. Soon, there were many girls gushing out of the dorm to search for sockets. After all, some had to talk to their caring boyfriends, some to their caring families, some to their possessive devils in the guise of boyfriends who would start imagining their girl sleeping with someone else if she didn't keep her phone reachable and answerable, and some with flirtatious and not so committed boyfriends whose insecure girls were worried about what their guys might be doing without them.

Leaving my phone and charger in the custody of the kind receptionist, I took a casual stroll to the gate. Ooty at 8.00 p.m. is almost like 1.00 a.m. in Kolkata – serene, cold, beautiful, but with tall trees, fresh air and the biting mist. While returning to the portico, I saw two devil eyes glowing as bright as molten lava near a bush. I ran till the portico, my heart beating. As I heard a 'meow' behind me, I realized that it was a black cat that I had seen in the dense, dark night. Oops! I stumbled after tripping over a pebble, but a strong hand caught me just before I hit the ground

I tried to recognize the face of my saviour in the dim blue light of the portico. I saw that it was Prakrit's. By now, his dress sense had improved a lot and he looked decent. He was a good looking chap.

"Thank you," I said to him. "I tripped on that stone."

"Chill. Tell me what happened before that," he asked.

"Nothing happened. What could happen? Nothing," I said, gasping for breath.

"The black cat scared me too," he said and grinned.

"Oh, that. Did you see me do all that – see it, get scared and run and fall down?" I asked embarrassed.

"Unfortunately yes, considering this was your awkward moment, and fortunately yes, considering it could have been a dangerous moment if I hadn't caught you," he said.

"Alright. Thank you again," I said.

"Most welcome. These are rare instances where I could be of help to the girl I admire," he said.

"Thanks. Hey, let's go inside before people get ideas and gossip about us," I said.

"I hope they get ideas and those turn into reality," he said not breaking his gaze thrown at me.

Though I didn't understand a word of it, I didn't find it necessary to ask. His words were Latin and Greek to me. It's such a human thing – that when you like someone, you scan the entire web, dictionary, thoughts and ask people again and again to understand and analyse the meaning of their words. And when it's someone who doesn't matter to you, you don't give it a second thought. For me, it was nothing. Just that some kind of compassion had emerged within me for him as he had saved me from the blind fall. I might have gone into a coma from that fall, who knows!

The next day, we went to the botanical garden in the morning. It was a lavish spread of green carpets of grass over hectares of land against the backdrop of majestic, endless mountains. One can find rare, beautiful as well as common species of plants, trees, herbs, shrubs, flowers in this seemingly unending park. I got lost in the beauty of nature. I stopped a batch-mate from dirtying the place with his cookie wrapper. I threatened to upload a video of his in the act if he threw the wrapper in the protected area even after my warning. This ensured that he located a bin and discarded the wrapper there. Priyanka and I posed in front of the India map formed with green plants like the characters in the movie *Titanic*, with our arms spread out to either side and took photographs.

After the park tour, we boarded the bus to visit the Pykara waterfalls. During the bus tour, I was spaced out. I was too captivated by the beauty of the hill station and it constantly distracted me from my friends. I could see the mesmerizing tea plantations, hills, birds, and smell the cold and subtly medicinal eucalyptus in air. We reached the entrance gate to the waterfall, and the guide at Pykara falls told us about the magnificent water body – that it is one of the oldest hydro electric power plants in South India and is still functional. Priyanka and I were the first ones to get out of the bus. As we walked towards the water, I saw a board with a warning: *'Enjoy the water with your eyes. Immersing your feet inside it is at own risk.'*

"Chuck it," Priyanka said.

"Let's go. I can't wait to get inside the water." I screamed. My being a Piscean could be attributed to my fondness towards water. I feel at peace when I see and touch this God's greatest gift to mankind.

"No, wait!" Priyanka said, but before she could say anything more, I ran to the stream. I tip-toed from one stone to the other and soon, was standing in the middle of the running water, calling out to Priya. "Hey take a photo of me, please."

"Noya, Noya, Noya, Noyaaaaaa…Oh my god…this girl… what is she up to?" Soon I heard the horrified voices of all my friends standing on the bank. "Come back." Priyanka screeched at the top of her voice.

"Why are you scared? I'm fine and enjoying myself. Why don't you join me?" I shouted back waving my hands.

"Mad girl, come back... Please, someone help her! Please!" Priya screamed and fainted.

As I put forth my leg to rush to her aid, I realized there was no stepping stone. Wasn't there a big stone a few minutes ago? I looked at Priyanka and now I understood why she had been hysterical. She loved me so much. All my friends stood there, clueless, some trying to call for help, some screaming. And then I looked back, and saw the water rising like waves of the ocean. I have never seen a waterfall so furious. I closed my eyes and thought about what my last wish was going to be. I apologized to my parents for the careless blunder for which I was going to lose my life. I suddenly missed them and tears filled my eyes. I prayed to God saying that I didn't want to die. I have so many dreams and I couldn't die before I fulfilled those.

Thud!

I heard a sound and felt a slimy thing around my legs. I shouted "Snake, snake, snake!" swiftly lifting my legs turn by turn.

"No, you stupid girl. Don't waste time. Just hold onto the rope and try to float across." I heard a voice.

"But I don't know how to swim!" I said while holding the rope.

"For now, just hold onto to the second knot of the rope and cling onto it till you find some human hand. Whatever happens, just don't let go. This rope is your life. Now stop looking at me and hold on to it!" Prakrit screamed.

"Okay Prakrit." I grasped the rope and jumped from the stone. It was a leap of faith. The faith bestowed on God. Another underlying hard stone bruised my knee. "Ouch" I played Prakrit's words over in my head: "Just don't let go".

"Am I alive?" One hand touched my nose to see if there was any breath of life and the other was on my chest, checking for a sign of a heart beat.

I was alive.

"I'm alive." I rejoiced.

I shouted as I sat up on the white bed sheet. I looked around at the white walls of the cabin. Priyanka was sitting beside me with my parents, both of whom looked tired and relieved. They looked like parents who have just seen their newborn child.

Yes, it was a new life for me. I was reborn that day. Prakrit had given me a second life.

I looked up at the bright, glittering chandeliers shining on the ceiling of the ritzy hotel where my parents had thrown a party as a thanksgiving and had invited my friends, professors and acquaintances from college.

I cringed at the sight of them doting on Prakrit. It was no wonder he was the hero of the day, but inside I felt something was not right. In their heightened pampering of him, I could also see how much they loved me. After the party, I went to Priyanka's house to drop her. She was still in trauma and had lost her bubbly self after that dreadful incident. She seemed to be more traumatized than me.

On reaching home, before opening the front door, I heard a voice talking to my mother. "No aunty, it is enough. You don't have to thank me anymore." Prakrit had reached my home. But he deserved all the attention. After all, I was indebted to him for bringing me back to my world.

"Hey Noya, Prakrit is going to stay here tonight. It's late, so we brought him along with us as his house is very far from the hotel," Mom said as I entered the living room.

"As you wish, Mom," I said.

"Raghu, take sahab to the guest room upstairs and see to it that he settles. Give him some clothes from the almirah in the guest room," Mom directed.

"Okay, this way," said the stout, strong and grey-haired housekeeper.

Just as I was falling asleep, I woke up to a notification sound and vibration on my phone. It was a text from Prakrit. I opened my tired and heavy eyelids which badly needed rest.

'Awake?' The text read.

I considered not replying; he would assume that I was fast asleep. How was he supposed to know that I did have a look at his text and ignored it? But a part of me chastised me that it was due to him that I was hale, hearty and alive.

'Yes. Anything you need?' I typed.

'On your terrace. Need to talk. Pl come upstairs.'

'Ok. In five,' I replied.

'Ok. Waiting.'

I quickly put on a pair of black track pants and wore a shrug to cover the spaghetti straps of my top.

I saw him sitting in one of the eight marble chairs surrounding the oval gem-studded table. He was drinking red wine, which he had taken from the bar-fridge on the terrace

"Do you want some?" he offered me the bottle.

"No, I don't drink," I said

"I'm shocked that with all the exotic drinks available in your house, you don't drink." He said sarcastically.

"Each person has their own preferences and choices. We should respect it." I jabbed back.

"Noya. How do you find me ?" His voice was now different with the impact of the alcohol he had consumed.

"Thanks for saving me. No favour can be enough in exchange of the life you have given me. So I thank you with all my heart. And I'm too tired. I'm going back to my room. I need sleep," I said.

"No. Wait. Okay, no beating around the bush. I like conversations which are true, direct, upfront and straight from the heart," he said.

I didn't like his tone – in fact I never liked anything of his ever except that he had sprung me, which in itself was a big thing.

"Noya," he said, walking closer to me. His breath bubbling with the smell of the alcohol.

I moved back, he came closer, I moved further back, he came closer further, I moved back till I hit the railing of the terrace and I could no longer use the space behind me. Now I felt something would happen which wouldn't be appropriate. Girls do have a sixth sense – a special power given to them by God to safeguard them. But sometimes, we trust our hearts more than the sixth sense and fall into a mess.

"I love you," he said. I felt a thousand knives piercing me. I was terrified. I didn't feel this way when the others had proposed to me. I had politely turned down their proposal.

"But I don't," I said in response. It was a quick reflex action. It seemed as if I already knew that he would say this and what my answer would be.

"But I love you a lot. I loved you from the day I saw you sitting in the auditorium. Then I tried sitting near you to get to know you more, but I couldn't gather the courage to talk to you. So I thought I would start avoiding you so as to control the feelings inside me." He went on.

I stood there dumbfounded. This was anticipated yet unexpected. The bright, rude, gruff Prakrit was standing in front of me and was proposing to me in my own home. Unbelievable.

"I need time to think. I will give you my response tomorrow," I said and came to my room and threw myself into my bed.

I need time to think. I will give you my response tomorrow. I recollected the crap I had spoken a minute back. When I was so sure that I didn't love him, why the hell did I say that? I felt as though I was falling into some trap. I knew I said that just to escape the situation.

The next dawn wasn't the usual one. I only got out of bed late at noon, though I had woken up early in the morning. I didn't feel energetic. When I checked my mobile phone, it had twenty texts from him.

Ten proclaimed his love for me, five were some 'see and forward' inspirational messages, and five asked me to meet him at the coffee shop near my house at six that evening.

'Meet me today at six. at the coffee shop, the one near your house.'

'Don't say no, please. I haven't closed my eyes for a second since last night.'

'Waiting to meet you as minutes tick by. Even the seconds feel like long eras.'

'Wear a red top when you meet me. You look cute in red.'

'Are you angry? Why no reply? I'm having panic attacks. Pl reply. I will be waiting at 6.00 p.m. even if you don't reply.'

I wasn't myself the entire day. I just kept staring at the ticking clock. All my profanities did not slow it down and soon it struck the numeral five, that was when I received another text from him:

'If you don't come down, I will come to your home. Whoever travels to meet the other doesn't matter, what matters is that we meet.'

Aargh! What the heck. Why was he suddenly texting me like this? I hadn't given this person any rights to bother me. I understood he had saved my life but that didn't mean he started behaving like the owner of my soul. I was still the owner of myself.

'Will be there at 6:00 p.m. Wait for me.' I texted with exasperation, my breath pacing its speed ten times.

I wanted to resolve all this and end the drama, so I started getting ready and reached the cafe. He was already seated there at the corner table near the pillar, a secluded corner away from the crowd.

He rose when he saw me me arriving and called the servitor to take our food order. I was kind of scared seeing his intense face. I sat opposite him and placed my handbag on the table.

"So. What have you thought about us?" he said while twitching his nose.

"Us! We were never meant to be together. Get lost." My mind screamed inside.

I cleared my throat and started the rehearsed lines. The harrumphing didn't help and I felt a lump in my throat.

"Listen, Prakrit. I pondered over it all night and all day. I know I owe you something in exchange of my life, but I realized that it can't be love as I don't have any such feelings for you. Apart from love, just ask anything else and I'm ready to give it to you," I said looking straight into his eyes.

His expression changed in an instant – his eyes narrow, his face grim, his tone quivery.

"I can understand that you need time and I don't know what has happened to me. I'm just immersed in your love," saying this, he burst into unrestrained tears. He said this while making no effort to wipe off the tears falling down his cheeks and into his cup of coffee. I handed over a tissue to him. The stares of the crowd around made me all the more conscious.

"Please stop, please.. for my sake.. don't cry," I said in panic.

"What should I do now?" he said.

"Ask me anything else," I said.

"Be my girlfriend," he said.

"How can I when I don't love you! Please understand me," I said.

"Be my girlfriend, without love, for a month. Know me. We shall be friends. If you don't fall in love, then we will part ways a month from today," he said.

"Are you out of your senses?" I said alighting from the chair, lifting my handbag. He stood in an instant and held my hand.

"You owe me that, don't you? I have given you a new life," he said strongly.

I don't know why, but it did hit me at the right place. Spot on. He got what he wanted.

"Okay. Just to satisfy your thoughts, I agree. Just because you have saved me and I stand here because of you," I said this, thinking there was no harm in telling him on the thirtieth day that I didn't develop any feelings. And I knew I did never ever have any kind of mushy feelings for him. I was only doing it for his sake.

That night, I just tossed and turned without any trace of sleep. The next morning, I had prominent dark circles beneath my eyes due to the insomnia, which had become my best friend these days. Best friends never leave you, no matter what!

I removed the portraits from the blue wall in front of my bed and put a huge calendar on it.

I drew a circle around the previous day's date, the 29th of May to mark the date on which this detrimental deal was made and I put another circle around the 27th of June.

I also took out a packet of cotton rounds which I used every night to use my facial toner. It will serve the dual purpose – for my daily regime and for count of the days, as the pack had 30 such cotton wipes.

What a hectic and noxious month this would be. I had just escaped death, then this deadly deal had been made and then the final exams too would begin the day after and I had not studied a word. I locked myself in my room to study for the exams.

While I was turning to page 1043 of the *World Economic History,* my cell phone beeped.

'My baby. Whats up?' It was Prakrit's. Then another message came, then another and so on…

I changed the notification setting to silent. After two hours of focused studying, I checked my phone again. There were thirty-six texts: two from Priya, one from Ayan and thirty-three from that idiotic maniac saviour of mine. I panicked and wanted to vent out my frustration. So I went to the gym room and walked on the treadmill for half an hour and also did a bit of kickboxing. It was all so weird that a girl so strong physically is so vulnerable mentally. It was all just because he had saved me. I would have preferred to have died that day if I would have known I would be bound to this fellow! Am I bonded labour? I knew I can just talk to my parents upfront about him, revealing all that he has done, and walk away from this disturbance. But something inside was restricting me in doing so. I wanted to handle it myself.

"Mom and Dad, from now on, do not entertain Prakrit. I understand he has saved my life and you kind of feel indebted to him but whatever we have done till now is enough. Let's not stretch it anymore," I said to them, while we were having dinner together.

"But dear, he saved you. No gratitude to him will be ever enough for us. What happened? Why are you sounding so low?" Mom asked, sounding concerned.

I didn't feel the time was appropriate to share anything with my parents. I also had my exams to deal with, so I thought I would park this discussion for later.

"Nothing. I'm going back to studying. Please send a cup of coffee to my room Mom," I said and returned to my room for studying. And I kept my disturbing phone in the drawer.

I woke up the next morning with Mom banging on my door. "Noya, Noya, open the door. Prakrit is here to meet you. He wants to talk to you about something important."

What the hell! He had reached my home again. How easy it was for him to gain access to my house, my family, my room – surpassing the security, the staff, the cameras, the dogs. He also could manage to convince my parents. If only I could turn back time.

"Why aren't you replying to any of my messages or calls? I got so worried that I rushed to your house today. I wanted to make sure you were fine," he rapped after mom left the room.

"This is just day one of our agreement and you have already started intruding in my life. I think we should give each other some privacy and space else it will never move in any direction," I said loudly showing my annoyance and disgust.

"But I was worried," he said, his eyebrows bent to a frown.

"Okay, but please don't do this from now on. I will respond to your calls and texts. And you have to understand that we have exams from tomorrow. So you have to study for it and also let me study. Live and let me live," I said gritting my teeth.

"I'm sorry if it hurt you but I expect you to be a bit more responsive from now. I will contact you after a week. But these seven days won't be counted as part of our agreement, I will extend the end-date of our deal by seven days," he said.

Was this a business deal? We never signed any legal document so on what basis was he after my life? Anyway, I was least interested in what he was saying and more interested in his exit from my room, from my house, from my life as soon as possible. His presence suffocated me. His dominating behaviour was making me miserable all the more.

"Okay, I accept. So bye for now," I said trying to sound stern and irritated. But he was least affected by my rudeness. All he wanted was my interaction, least bothered by the underlying feelings. What I felt or needed didn't bother him.

I pulled aside the curtain I had put over the newly mounted private calendar and put seven crosses on it. I was relieved that seven days would pass without any interference from him.

My exams did not go that well, but I had at least managed to study to make it to a first division. On the eighth day of the month, after the exams, while I was partying with my friends, I received a text.

'How did your exams go? See, I stuck to my commitment. I never disturbed you – neither in college nor your home nor through phone or mails. Am I not a good boy?'

What a daunting haunting text. It just turned my world upside down in a jiffy.

"Hey babe, what happened to your smile? Come and dance. Leave your phone," Rima said.

I quickly wrote, '*At a party. Contact you later. Don't text till then.*' and switched off my phone.

The next morning, I decided to leave the place. If you can't change the other person, better change the situation. Only the change of situation is in your control, not the person.

"Dad and Mom, I want to work. Not in our family business, but some other salaried corporate job," I said, thinking that if I were to go away from this place, I would be going away from him.

"Have we ever denied you anything? Do what you feel like, whatever you want," Dad said while giving me a high five.

After registering my profile on ten job sites, I applied for one hundred and six vacancies, non-stop. And luck favoured me, I got a job call within two hours.

"Hello, is this Noya? We are calling from ZA Associates. This is in reference to your job application posted on searchnaukri.com," said a grave voice.

"And which location is the job based in?" I asked in anticipation, lifting myself from the chair. I badly wanted the job.

"Kolkata. So don't worry, as you don't have to leave your home-town." The voice answered with a chuckle.

"Oh, in that case, I'm very sorry. In fact, I'm looking for a location other than Kolkata. So please let me know in case you have any such opportunity," I said disheartened, with my hopes shattered.

"I'm surprised. But alright, I will get back if there is any such opportunity," he said and disconnected the call.

After another hour, my phone buzzed again.

"Hello, is this Noya? This is Raman from ZA Associates. I called you an hour ago. I discussed your case with our manager. You will be glad to know that we have recently opened a new branch in Jamshedpur. So if you agree, you can join us there."

"Alright. When is the joining date? Can I join day after?" I said with a squeak of relief, seeing that the turn of events was how I expected.

"Oh it's nice to see that you are so eager to join us! You may join us day after. Coincidently, we have a batch joining day after. So you can have an induction together. I will send you the offer letter, checklist and forms tomorrow. Please arrange for your tickets. We will refund the cost you incur," he said.

"Mom and Dad, I got a job. It is in Jamshedpur. That is nearby so you don't have to worry. I will be fine. And I will have to leave tomorrow. I need to complete the induction formalities and medical check-up," I said while having a mixed bag of emotions – sad, happy, strong, relieved, determined.

Jamshedpur, here I come, I thought as I clambered down from the train at the railway station. The bumpy ride on the road from the railway station to the town made me wonder an umpteen number of times whether I had taken the right decision – but right or wrong, it was a necessitated decision.

That day, I checked into the company's guest house. Then proceeded for the medical check-up at the hospital. In the evening, I went around to get acquainted with the place – the market, the park, the restaurants. I had a relaxed sleep in the night. Next morning, we were to report at the office.

I entered the conference room of ZA Associates for the induction and sat amongst the most professional looking guys in suits and ties. I wondered if I was the only girl here. From the time I had entered the office to this moment, I hadn't seen any other girl. And then someone came scurrying in.

"Oh, sorry sir, I got late by a minute," she said. "And I'm Disha," she added, introducing herself. We exchanged smiles and I signalled that she was late by ten minutes and not a minute.

After the presentations and speeches, we were briefed on our roles and responsibilities. My clients were in Innovation Steel – the company being major players in the steel business. From dealing with production of steel, giving back to the society, doing social work, providing jobs, they were a firm with interests in a variety of areas.

"So you go to Innovation Steel and meet Mr Harshit. He is your customer. He will brief you on what reports and information they require from you as part of our contract."

"All right." On my way, as I approached the Innovation Steel community area, I realized how beautiful Jamshedpur was with stretched trees and vast lawns on both sides of the road, bright bungalows tucked neatly in a row and the roads sparkling clean without a speck of dirt or visible waste. The place and the inhabitants looked happy and content.

I reached the premises of the Innovation Steel plant, showed my permit, signed the ledger and entered the Finance and Accounts department. After asking for directions from a number of people, I reached the required workplace.

"Hey Noya...blab bla bla... la la la... and this is Prakrit Raj, the new employee who has joined us today. Though you won't have any working relationship with him, I thought I would introduce you since you both are from the same college," Harshit said.

What... What...What...what did he just say? I was already having initial pangs of a panic attack inside me. God let it not be him. Let it be some other Prakrit Raj, though I didn't know any other in my college. It just can't be him – my mind was screaming inside and my heart wanted to come out of the body. I turned towards the door to look at the person Harshit was pointing at.

And there he stood – the monster. It was him!

"Harshit, we both already know each other. We are good friends but we are meeting after a long time. Hey let's go and eat some snacks. They have a good canteen," Prakrit said as he held my hand and steered me.

"Check out this canteen, it offers good food at subsidized rates. Isn't it a great thing? Just imagine – a plate of idli at five bucks or a dosa at ten. Who said you can't have stomach filling lunches just for ten rupees?" he asked, seemingly joyous. He had no clue what was I feeling at that moment – pathetic, unfortunate, cursed, doomed. Nor did he bother to look into my eyes and explore my emotions, given the cold being he was.

"How come you are here, and you never told me?" I managed to mumble.

"It was you who told me not to contact you. Moreover, though I was not in touch with you, I was in touch with your Mom. I had this offer from the company but I hadn't decided whether to join or not, but the moment I got to know from your mother that you would be coming here, I thanked the Lord for giving me this offer. I'm so so happy. We are here, together. Isn't this an indication that we are made for each other? How much more time do you need to understand this?" he said while eating a chunk of that five rupee idli, dipped in sambhar and chutney.

I was destined to fall in love with him. They say when you really long for something from your heart and aspire to have it with your whole being, the entire universe conspires to get it for you. I believe Prakrit wanted me badly and so he got me.

I was in love. This wasn't those puppy love crushes but a committed relationship. After all that he had done for me – waiting for me for endless hours, till I left office, to accompany me home and ensure I reached safely; going shopping with me whenever I wanted to; protecting me from stalkers; cooking for me and bringing the food in a tiffin so that we could have lunch together; talking daily and sharing how the day passed – all this eventually made me develop feelings for him. Though something deep inside me was shouting that he was not the right guy for me, I still wanted to give it a try, for the sake of his love for me. I fell for him. And soon, I too was in love with him. It was 'us' and 'together' now. He had changed and now he was a caring, loving boyfriend.

Prakrit was very keen on marrying me as soon as possible. With each passing day, he was getting more and more impatient. Every conversation of his led to marriage talks.

"But we are only twenty-four." I reminded him while splurging into the choco-chips sundae sitting on the bench of a jogging park, attempting to buy some more time.

"You will be twenty-five in two months. It isn't any big deal. My mother married when she was eighteen."

"To be honest, I'm still in a tender age. I don't think it's the right age to marry. We still need some more time to understand each other before taking the plunge."

"Alright." He said sensibly and left after dropping me home.

In the evening, he called me home. I reached the place and he was waiting for me near the door. Once inside, he held my hand and cried profusely.

"Noya, you don't trust me even now."

"I do."

"Then marry me." He went on persistently, shedding buckets of tears.

How can one see the tears of the one they love.

"Alright we will think about it. Now smile." I said wiping tears off his flushed cheeks.

"Yay. My Noya agreed for tying the knot," and he rushed to his phone and the next second, I heard him telling his mother, "She agreed Mom. Let's fix up the meeting."

Did I agree for it? Nevertheless I could not conflict his joy. One day I have to marry, so let it be, I told myself. Dates were planned for the rendezvous of the two families.

As both the breeds sat and discussed, I observed a total mismatch - one was the sophisticated lot, that talked in refined language; the other one was crude, that never thought once before blurting out a word. His family was more occupied in checking out the bungalow, the cars, the artefacts, and the other's business. Date of the wedding was fixed for next month. After they left, my mother came to my room and asked again, "You saw his family. Are you sure about marrying him? We won't force you in your decision, but something inside is making me feel he is not the right guy for you. Will you be able to adjust in that household? Are you sure?"

"You are so sweet Mom. I'm sure about marrying him and he is a nice boy. I trust him. And after all, marriages come with the share of adjustments and compromises. If I'm not ready to budge a bit for my love, won't I be selfish." I said, pretending to be normal, while inside me there was an ocean at panic. But I trust him. He would take care of everything. We loved each other.

"You sound like a septuagenarian. You have grown so much, in statistics, in mentality, in wit. Love you, my child. We will miss you." She hugged me and we cried loads that night.

"Priyanka, I'm getting married." I screamed into the phone.

"Are you sure. I'm not excited. Neither was I when you got into a relationship with him, nor I am today. But I will attend your wedding. Don't worry. Just for you."

"My wedding is fixed, guys. Keep your dates free. No excuses." I informed my friends Rima, Ayan, Rohan, and Kriti whom I put on a conference call.

"And you expect us to get surprised and shout ooh lala. It won't be. For god's sake, you are just twenty-four. Couldn't you both wait for a couple of years? What's the urgency to cross the line of virginity," Rima roared.

"After seeing you, our parents will put you as example in all our conversations and will be behind our asses. I will have a tough time defending myself," Rohan screamed.

"You still have time. Think well and take the plunge," Ayan said.

Everyone asked Kriti what she felt, because she had been quiet all this while. "I'm shocked. No words. May God bless you," Kriti said.

"Stop it guys. The reality is I'm getting married and you can't change it. I'm so excited. Lots of work to do and so less time. I will split the tasks amongst you and send you via mail. Start working on them," I said taking over from them.

My house was on budge at its extreme with all the planning, communication, and preparation work ongoing. I did expect that my parents would go over the top in their preparation so every now and then, I had to remind them to keep the wedding a simple affair as I didn't want anything going too extravagant and overboard. When I shared this with Prakrit, he said, "You are the sole daughter. Let them do what they want and how they wish." We argued on the topic but never reached a consensus.

Everything was going as per plans when that day came which ruined it all. That day I regretted having known Prakrit at all. It was four days before the wedding. The cards had been sent out. The venue was booked. The caterers informed. There were hordes of relatives and friends hovering at my place. My dreams of a future with him had increased ten-fold. I was getting ready with the tingling thoughts of the moments when I would become one with him.

Another dawn and the atmosphere at my home had changed. I saw my parents and relatives tensed but when asked, they did not share anything with me and gave only lame excuses. That was when I overheard my parents talking.

"They are demanding money, a house and a car. This we were anyways gifting. But we were giving these out of care and love to our daughter and son-in-law. But it's not the goods that is worrying me, but the attitude of their family. How can I let my daughter go to a home that is still open to such thoughts? How will she adjust there?" Dad was bleakly telling mom.

"Yes, I understand. But she loves him. How can we break her heart? I'm confused. Give me some time. Let me think whether we should inform her or just carry on," Mom replied holding his hand.

I barged in wasting no second, "How could you even think of hiding this from me?"

❖

"Prakrit, how can your parents speak to my parents like this? Hadn't I made it clear that there won't be any such thing in our marriage?" I yelled at him.

I expected a sensible reply. Instead, he just remained calm, worriless, thoughtless, virtue-less. The only words he spoke were, "This is common. Why are you throwing a tantrum about it? My brothers had sought and sisters had given during their marriages. Moreover, where is the money going? It will come back to us only."

When he said this, my heart crunched and cringed within me. This was the kind of person I was getting into an alliance with. Why had I let myself into this mess? I know all the blame goes to myself – the sole culprit for the state of affairs. He wasn't the same person I had known from my college days. At least the earlier personality had some shades of love and care. This one was only greedy.

It was just three days before the big day and I lay confused on my bed. In the midst of the trauma, I kept myself determined and sane. I had resorted to most of the techniques mentioned in the self-help books, blogs, sites, counselling from friends and family – meditation, chanting mantras, thumbing the rudraksha string, looking forth to a palate of life goals. At times, I decided I couldn't let my life be in the hands of a couple of halfwits, but then, I loved him. I felt weak too. I knew what was right and what was wrong. But I loved him.

"Will you talk about this to your parents or not?" I asked him, again with the hopes that maybe I had been mistaken yesterday.

"They are elder to me. How can I go against my parents? Why are you creating a ruckus out of it?" He answered in his crude tone.

"At the cost of our love and relationship?" I asked him.

"I know you love me and you will be a fool if you do any such foolish thing. What will society say? Who will marry a girl who has her wedding called off days before it?" he answered.

"How could I not see through the person you are actually inside. You are right that I'm a fool." I said and disconnected the call. I avoided all his follow-up calls and texts. I just expected one apologetic message from him, but it never arrived.

Two days before marriage, I called him and again gave him a chance. "What have you thought? Does your stand remain what it was yesterday?"

"Yes. Things will be good after marriage. Don't worry. This money and house is for us. So how does it matter who finances it? Your parents' money is yours ultimately. So what's the big deal?" he said without any remorse in his voice.

"If things aren't good before marriage, then they will never be after that too. Its not the money and house that matters. It's the respect and self respect that does. I hope you understand this one day," I replied.

"I'm your husband. Don't you talk to me in that manner." He said coarsely, raising his voice like he had never done.

"You are not my husband yet. And I will make sure that my husband doesn't talk to me in this manner. I don't deserve this." I reminded him.

"Any change in you?" I asked him a day before the marriage too.

"Why should I change? I'm good enough for you. I have better grades than you. I earn better than you. I look better than you. You are getting more than you deserve. Don't you tell me to change ever." He snapped.

"Thanks Prakrit. Cause your words made me realize what I had overlooked earlier. I may not be what you told me now, but I'm a human. I'm kind, soft, sensitive, honest and proud of it. And it's true that I don't deserve you," I said, this time sure of what I deserved.

On the day of the marriage, I sat on the wedding mandap in a dazzling maroon and golden lehanga, with heavy thread, sequin, semiprecious stone work. I myself had designed it and had monitored its daily progress. I waited for my groom – my 'supposed to be hubby' Prakrit Raj. I recalled how my life wired me from college to the tunnels of love to marriage. I clinched my fist cursing myself for the blunder. But mistakes are your own choices. Such faux pas are learning which you must sense, move on and never repeat.

I was sitting there, awaiting his arrival. He would reach after dancing in the baraat, a part of Indian marriage ceremony where the groom, his family, friends, near and dear ones come in a procession to the wedding venue.

I called him up, but when he didn't attend, I called his cousin and requested to give the phone to him.

"Any change in your views?" I asked him with bated breath. "Please behave good." I thought to myself.

"Are you insane? You expect me to attend your call while I'm in a baraat. Couldn't you just wait for an hour." He rushed.

"I need an answer. What if I don't fulfil your demands? Won't you marry me? I asked.

"I will." He said, making me shut my eyes in relief and shedding a tear. This is what I wanted to hear all this while.

"Hello. Can you hear me? There was a signal problem and my talk got interrupted. I will marry you. But before our marriage, please keep the items ready. My parents have detained me and are forcing that I should only go to the mandap if the stuff is agreed and ready." He ranted, leaving me shocked. I had enough on my plate now and could not tolerate anymore. I was done.

He was now slowly revealing true colours just like a perfume would spill up its fragrances gradually - at first its top notes then the middle and next the base. He was at his base nature now – the real him.. Nothing seemed to get inside his mind. He was too adamant and greedy. I wondered where was the love which he had once claimed. People do change or maybe he was like this all the time. His love was not for me, but for my financial affluence.

A mile away, Prakrit must have thought to himself that soon they would tie the knot and then he would have the legal license to devour her, further control her life, gain some lucky money and property, and have children.

As they entered the hall, they were in shock. Noya was standing near the entrance with a garland. This was not it. She was in a t-shirt and chinos.

"What's this? On this day, you are embarrassing us in front of our friends and relatives. Go and get dressed," Prakrit's father screamed. His mother went scurrying to their relatives and chanting excuses to cover up the scene.

"What's this?" Prakrit said, holding me tight by my arm.

"It's you who said that you won't change. So I decided that I too won't change," I replied.

"Dad, I won't marry such a freaky girl. Let's go back," he chortled.

"Well, Mr Prakrit. I say no to marrying you. Before you came, we communicated to our guests that there is an issue and the marriage has been postponed. But the next time it happens, it won't be you in it. And we had a scrumptious feast and celebrated my fortunate escape." I informed.

"You can't do this to me and my family. I saved you. We are about to get married now. God has plans for us," Prakrit said.

"God does make people meet. But ultimately it's our actions that decide who is to stay and who is to leave. Since the time I got to know your intentions, I've been leading a life of suffocation. I feel someone has put a plastic bag over my head and held it tightly and I'm unable to breathe normally. And God has not created this life for me; I myself have. It was my choice. But now, I won't repeat the mistake. I know what I want," I said.

He went out for a while and the family had a discussion and then he entered again. He held my hand, bent on his knees and asked for forgiveness. His parents followed and apologized. But now I was sure of what I wanted. I wanted to break free from such laggards, such mentalities.

"Prakrit, enough! Do you and your parents have an ounce of self-respect? Anyway, I'm walking out of this relationship. I got hooked to you because you had saved me. And you came close to me using your pretentious tactics. I was a fool that I loved you. I can no longer be a fool for the feelings inside me towards you. And you will never understand these feelings. You have never really loved me. I was an obsession for you. For you, I was a gold mine. Now I understand why you wanted me so badly. I didn't trust your good-willed friend too, when he revealed your plans to me. My family and friends did caution me on this marriage, but I trusted you. I thought, can a person in love be bad? I thought you loved me. But you have changed to your best interests. I was dumb to have had any love for you. You don't deserve anything. I pity myself. But all that I want now is to walk away from the mistake," I said while trying my best to hold back my tears. I didn't want to seem like a weak person in front of these morons.

That day, I could not control myself any further and like a cloud which bursts into rain, I exploded at his parents.

"What kind of upbringing and education have you given your child who says dowry is common, who says emotional torture is discipline, who says staying grim is being mature? Manipulative, shrewd, cunning, dominating, adamant is what he has become," I screamed out like an approaching storm.

He stepped forward and gave me tight slap. "How dare you talk to my parents like this?"

"How dare you!" I punched him hard on his stomach. He didn't know yet that I was a champion in karate and kickboxing.

Till now, I had tried my best to be amiable and composed, but it was off the brim now.

"Just leave the place else I will call the police. Prakrit, you saved my life once. Today, I'm saving yours and your parents' by not calling the cops. We're even! And one more thing - real men don't sell themselves, and wise women don't buy defective pieces."

I made myself strong and wise to discard all their pleas, cries and apologies thereafter. It was hard, especially when you still have feelings of love within you for the person. But one should do what's right, not just blindly follow what's easy. That was the day I boarded the train at Howrah station.

Living with him was like always living in a hazy narcosis – accepting a fake life and pretending that it was my life. I wanted to get through these murky moments without realizing where my crumpled life was leading me. I did aspire for an eternal love but not to be trapped in the eternity of this never-ending desperation for freedom. Each moment of my life was made up of panting, ranting, fighting, misunderstanding, tolerating. I didn't have a single moment when I felt content or happy. Let alone this, I had forgotten to smile, to eat, to read, to talk, to live. I deserved to be someplace else.

All this while, when I was speaking, my eyes were on the table and my hands callously stirring the drink. I then saw the time on the watch I was wearing.

"God, it's late. I have to rush to my friends. They are staying the night at a friend's house," I screamed.

"Tell them you will be late," Ranbir said with a persuasion in his voice. "I want to be with you for some more time."

"No, I can't. I have to leave," I insisted but when my eyes moved up and looked into his, there was something in his eyes which directed me to stay back and not rush. His cheeks and ears turned red.

"Rima, please tell everyone that I have met Ranbir and so I will be late. I will be with him for a while," I called her up and said.

"All right, baby. But please take care and hang around with him only in a public space," she said with concern.

"Thanks, love. I know that and I will. Don't you worry dear," I said in response to her. "And I don't have to fear when he is around anymore. I trust him." I whispered, cautious to not let him hear.

"What a maniac and devil he was!" he said, his eyes filled with tears.

"How could he behave in such a manner with you? With a girl who was supposed to be his partner for life? You did the right thing. You are brave. I hate such people who consider money above everything. Such people, who prioritize money, should toil hard to get money, not beg from others. And his pathetic parents…they should be…" he said and I stopped him by putting my hand over his mouth before he could say a swear word. I felt his quivering lips on my palm.

I was amazed to see what Ranbir was truly like. Only if I would have met him earlier. I felt I had lost precious moments of friendship by not having known him earlier.

"I don't want to think about my past anymore. This is my version. Maybe when you hear his version, you will find me the culprit," I said with an attempted smile to lighten up the situation.

But he banged his glass on the table and retorted, "You always have to be the charming girl. After all this, it is your greatness that you have not sent the mad family behind bars. Their deserving place is the prison, not your memories. They have no right to be anywhere near you anymore," he said while still trembling in anger. His legs vigorously shaking. His breath quick. His fingers restless. In all the time that I had known him for, I had never heard or seen him so angry.

To ease his mood, I told him to take me on a drive. He was quiet all the time. I was busy fiddling with the buttons on the music system.

After an hour or so, I looked at the watch and shrieked, "Let's go now. It's two. Time just flew. And what will your girl think if she gets to know that you were with another girl till this late?"

"Shut up. When will you grow up? I will drop you now. And we will never talk about your marriage again. I can't tolerate conversations about such maniacs...morons," he said sternly, in a tone to which I dared not reply.

But then I remembered that I had to check into a hotel as I didn't want to stay the night at Meera's place. The reason, more than my dislike towards her, was my state of mind. He left after I reached my room in the hotel.

Early the next morning, when I went to our rented house, I heard Rima shouting loudly at Rohan.

"How could you Rohan? How could you do this! I thought you were a sensible boy. Just because we are in a far off place, does this mean we forget our virtues?" she said, crying out loudly.

Rohan packed his bags and left in a hurry, trying to avoid meeting my eyes as well.

I ran to Rima and held her with one hand around her waist and another on her cheek. We went to the balcony. "What happened? Calm down. I'm here. Tell me what happened."

"That bastard slept with her yesterday," she said in angst, seething in the manner one would if one's diehard enemy is in front.

"Oh God. I knew she was like that. We shouldn't have increased our acquaintance with her," I said in shock.

"Yes. But he said she took him to the terrace of her house while all of us were asleep, and seduced him. He says he was drunk. But just because he was drunk, is it an excuse that I should forgive him? Any day he will get drunk again, does it mean he can do anything he wants and get away? Is he a baby that without his consent, she will carry him in her lap?" she said while a stream of tears flowed down her cheeks.

"Relax. Forgive him. We will counsel him," I said.

"How can I? That rascal had proposed to me day before yesterday and I had said I needed time to think and answer as I liked him as well. I wanted to give him an answer after discussing it with my family and you. You know me," she said angrily.

"It's better to realize the nature of the person before marriage, anyway. So take it as a fortunate sign from God that he showed you Rohan's true colour before any commitment. After a commitment, when you face the harsh reality, it hurts a lot more. And who knows it better than me," I said, remembering my spooky past.

"Yes, you are right. I'm lucky that I got to see one of his facets. Why am I the one who is crying? Fuck off Rohan," she said while bringing a smile to her freckled cheeks and showing a middle finger.

"I'm feeling strong now," she said. "I love you, baby."

She gave me a very tight hug and a kiss.

All of us spent the entire day with Rima, trying to make her forget the pain her heart had endured. At night, I excused myself and called Ranbir to enquire about his mood and shared what had happened with Rima. I had found a best friend in him. I felt like sharing everything with him as I knew they wouldn't be just words for him - he would be right there for me, for us, helping Rima heal her emotional wounds. He is a person who is genuinely concerned for people around him.

As expected, Ranbir called us to a party he had organised; he said he wanted us to meet Niti there. We all gathered at his house. That day, his family was out of station so we could not meet his parents.

"Where is Niti?" I asked him with my wandering eyes. My heart seemed to beat faster at the prospect of seeing the girl who was lucky to be spending her entire life with him.

"Oh, she texted me just now saying that she won't be able to come. She had to leave for her grandparents' home in Mumbai as her granny is not well," he said. "I wanted you to meet her so badly. Anyway, next time," he said while handing me a lemonade.

"Oh, so sorry to hear that," I said.

Ranbir left no efforts to look after Rima and make her feel special. He also consoled her. There was something magical in him, else Rima would not have gathered back her chirpy smile so soon after the episode.

After the party, Rima, Kriti, Ayan and I decided to take a walk along the beach to calm our senses.

As we were strolling, we heard some loud talks behind a big rock being hit by the waves.

We ignored them and kept walking until we heard, "Hey Rohan, how could she be such a jerk? I mean didn't you tell her it was just a one night stand. I'm about to get married. After that, you are hers entirely. This is so common these days. Aren't people allowed to have their own sexual preferences? How can you get into a relationship with such an old school girl?"

The voice paused, "Till you hit on another girl again." And they laughed.

"Don't worry, and don't spoil the mood by talking about this now. I know I can handle her. Some tears, some excuses of being drunk is all that's needed to make her accept my apologies. We will be fine. Now shut up and kiss me," the male voice said and sounded like the Rohan's we knew.

I signalled to the others to leave the place but Rima was adamant to know whether it was our Rohan or some other. So we hid behind the mangrove near the rock and waited till they consummated whatever they were doing and came out.

It was Rohan indeed. We could not see the girl as she had glares and a stole wrapped on her head. But we assumed if he was Rohan, then the girl must be her, following the conversation we overheard.

"That cheapster! This time I will kick his ass and his groin, where it will hurt him the most!" Rima said and was going to come out of our hideout. Ayan and I stopped her.

I put my hand on her rumbling mouth and said, "We should leave the situation as it is. Why should you care? I won't let you love him as he doesn't deserve you. I don't mind playing the villain here. So let's leave. It's no longer our concern."

The next day seemed hazy and dull, considering what had happened over the last few days. Kriti had to leave as she got a call from her parents that a prospective groom had come and she had to meet the boy and his family.

Ayan shared a deep secret with me; he told me that he loved Rima. When I asked him why he had flirted with Jenny, he said that he did it just to make Rima jealous. I suggested that he take Rima out and spend some time with her since she was in a dejected mood. I knew that if Rima could begin to develop feelings for Ayan, then they would be the best for each other; both were sweethearts. They both needed some time to heal their hearts. I thought of catching up with Ranbir and telling him that I wanted to meet Niti.

He agreed and told me to meet them at the Regal Cafe.

I reached the café but they were yet to arrive. I went to the washroom, and as I came out of it, I saw Meera sitting with two guys. I felt a thousand pricks inside me, instigating me to go and punch her; but she wasn't alone. And wondrously, she was behaving in a coy and subtle manner. She didn't seem to be the girl I knew. I changed my angle of vision a number of times to see her company and then I could see...*Ranbir!*

What the heck was happening to us? What on earth was this cursed, deceitful lady doing with Ranbir? She did not deserve to be talking to him.

Then I saw Ranbir fiddling with his phone and I heard a beep on my phone.

'Where are you? We are waiting for you.'

I understood the scene now. Ranbir was the boy whom Meera was to marry, while she had another guy she had plans to marry. There was also Rohan, the guy she had sex with. It was the first time I had got to know a girl like this – three-timing. I also deduced that Meera was her good name while Niti, her nickname, which she toggled and used to her advantage.

'Ranbir, I'm sorry that I'm telling you this late but I fell sick, and so I can't come. See you some other day,' I texted him.

It wasn't a complete lie – my head had started reeling and I felt as if I had serious positional vertigo. The uneasiness took over me. I felt I will pass out. I entered the washroom and splashed some cold water on my face.

'Okay, take care,' he replied and I watched them leave.

Back at home, after I narrated all that had happened, Ayan and Rima were equally shocked and concussed.

"I have to do something about her. I can't let her hurt someone for no fault of theirs. I have to reveal the ongoing scene to Ranbir before he falls into the trap," I said overcome with helplessness.

"But he is in love with her. Why would he trust us rather than her?" Rima said sensibly.

Ayan excused himself and soon he was back with sheets of big-sized paper, markers, pens and scales.

"What's this?" I asked.

"For our plans." He said.

"Throw them away. The best and most successful plans are not made on paper but in the mind. This is about lives. We can't leave any clue on paper," I said sounding like one of Sherlock Holmes's interns. After a lot of brainstorming and deliberation, we decided to keep the plan simple.

Rima suggested that we can call her over to stay with us. Ayan would be the bait; we would record the ongoing seduction and then show it to Ranbir. Given her nature, she would easily fall for the bait, since Ayan was rich and would promise her many a thing.

But after sharing the plan, and convincing Ayan after a lot of reluctance, Rima started getting apprehensive.

"Girl, I feel anxious. What if he turns out to be like Rohan after the seductress stint?" she whispered in my ears.

"If he too has morals like him, then it's good to throw him into testing waters and see if he wanders off too," I said in a detective like manner and convinced her.

"It's said all over the world that all men are dogs. But dogs are loyal. So it's time to check his loyalty, my royalty," I said.

"Alright. If you say so. For you. For me," she agreed.

I called Meera and invited her to stay the night saying that Rima had left and I was feeling lonely, but it turned out that she was busy that day. She also said she was going to her to-be in laws' home for the engagement. Her family had come down from Mumbai for the occasion.

Oh no! Engagement… today! And Ranbir hadn't even bothered to inform me. I felt a thousand billion knives were piercing inside me.

Change of plan! We had to do something quickly. We had to act fast. I couldn't knowingly allow Ranbir getting stuck in this crappy quicksand. I had to be his protector, his saviour.

Rima said, “Noya dear, we don’t have time. To save your friend, we have to do this – we will either find a way or make one.

“Here baby, drink this. I have prepared lemonade for you. Now, listen to the plan.” She said.

I gulped down the lemonade in four shots and asked for more. I needed more to quench my thirst that had arisen due to the nervousness inside me. While I drank three more glasses, Rima spoke.

“Rehearse these lines. ‘I love you, Ranbir. From the day I saw you on the train to Puri. That’s why I have come all the way from Kolkata to Goa. It is only for you. Marry me’.” Her words resounded in my ears and I felt numb.

Rima dressed me in a lehenga choli, dabbed some pancake make-up on my face and dropped me at the gate of Ranbir’s house.

I signed the ledger at the gate showing Ranbir’s texts and calls on my mobile as identity of myself to the reluctant guard, and reached the door. Through the glass, I saw Meera and a guy sitting on adjacent royal chairs and an elderly and a middle-aged couple standing on either side of them.

I entered with a bang.

“My baby. I love you. From the time I fought…” *What was I saying?* “…saw you. Your eyes, your behaviour and you are so captivating. Remember, you had promised to marry me. And that we will have lovely kids…”

Thud.

I fell down on the floor before I could complete the sentence.

As I partially opened my eyes, laying on the *dewan*, I could see that hordes of people were hovering over my head and staring at me.

There were murmurs all around.

"Who is she?"

"How can Ranbir do such a thing? She must have seduced him."

"But this girl is pretty and looks so decent!"

Another voice cut across, "How can such an innocent looking girl do such a thing?"

I loved the person who had called me 'innocent' and blew some imaginary kisses to her. I got up from the soft and comfortable dewan I was lying on and looked around for Ranbir. I saw him standing near the door and before he could say anything, Meera came rushing up with her parents.

She threw a horrible tantrum.

"Oh god, this is Noya. The girl who is trying to snatch the love of my life!" Meera said this wailing loudly. I was astonished to see her transformed so completely. Just the previous night, she had been kissing a boy and here she was claiming that Ranbir was the love of her life.

"Who is she? Just get her out of the house!" Meera's father shouted.

Ranbir's parents came running to the rescue as they knew me through Ranbir and he had probably informed them of my intoxication.

"There is some confusion. She is a good friend of Ranbir. She is drunk as we all can see. Let her come to her senses and then we talk." Ranbir's mother stood by my side.

"Girls like her just want rich boys like Ranbir and they can do anything to get them," Meera's mother taunted. "She is that divorcee girl my daughter was talking to me about. After one marriage, she has not learnt manners. She now eyes Ranbir."

"She isn't a divorcee. She just called off a marriage. I know the entire story. Nothing wrong with what she did." Ranbir's mother replied.

The entire hall started looking at me as if I'm some clown who has come down to entertain them on the big day.

I stood up and still there, looking for Ranbir.

He came to me, held my hand, and spoke haltingly, "She is my friend. Last night, she was at a party, and that's why she is in an intoxicated state. We had cooked up a prank for the guests. And so, she is narrating the rehearsed lines. But I guess she has consumed far too much alcohol than we had directed her to. Please ignore her. And don't say such harsh things about her. Let's get back to the engagement."

I was still swaying left and right with my vision blurring and my head spinning, so I held onto his arms. I was totally out of my senses now. He softly made me sit on a chair and signalled one of his sisters to take care of me till he gets free from the ring ceremony.

With my blurry vision, I realized they were exchanging rings and after that, Meera kissed his cheek.

"Congratulations!" I screamed and fainted again. Was it due to the impact of the alcohol mixed by Rima in the lemonade, or was it due to the shock I had received? Nevertheless, it was both to the extreme.

When I opened my eyes, I saw I was in the centre of a spotlessly clean, bright, shining room with four white walls and a small door with no knob on the inside. I felt Iight and weightless and I realized I was wearing no clothes but something like an apron… Oh no, it was a hospital gown and I was on a bed with glucose being induced to me. But I have fear of needles! Before I could process anything more, a nurse stepped inside.

"We saw you wake up and I came inside," she explained.

"But how did you know that I have woken up?"

"Oh, we have cameras fixed here and we continuously monitor the patients. But it's set in such a manner that we can only see the patient's face," she winked.

"Really, is it? Are the hospitals these days that advanced in technology?" I said.

No, no. It was a joke. It was my visiting time and it was a coincidence that you were up. How are you feeling now? Wait, I'm calling your friend who has been waiting the whole night in the waiting hall," she concluded, and went off.

The door opened. "Rima, you crazy girl, what did you mix in the delicious lemonade and make it deadly? See what has happened to me. Now people think I'm a maniac who is after a committed boy," I screamed angrily.

"Wait wait, hold on…hang on…it's me… Ranbir…the stalker… Recognize me?" He waved his hand at me.

"Where is Rima? And I can see you, Ranbir. I'm absolutely fine," I said embarrassed.

"She and Ayan were here last night but I told them that I wanted to stay here. I also thought I could give them some private time. And the doctor said you are mentally stable and it was just the intoxication. It seems you are not a regular drunkard. The amount of liquor in your body wasn't proportionate to your reaction though," he said, laughing.

Again his titters. "Excuse me. I did it all for you because Meera is a…" But I stopped as Rima's wise words came back in my whirling mind: "He will not believe whatever we say. We need to show him evidence – a photograph, video, on site, voice – whatever, wherever, whenever – but we need fact based records."

It did make sense. "Oh, that. I did that as I was intoxicated. And you yourself had said that you didn't love her yet, so I was trying to save you before you had to commit."

"That's it? And nothing else?"

"Yes, that's it and nothing else." I was delighted at my self-restraint which allowed me not to reveal such vital information.

"Noya, I wish it was something else..." he said, and gazed into my eyes for a long time.

"When am I getting discharged?" I broke his gaze. His vicinity and perfume had given me butterflies.

"Today, of course. You are here just because you have been repeatedly passing out, else it is nothing serious. Get back to your senses soon. I have a million questions."

"But I have no answers to your questions for now," I replied.

"But I ought to know the reason for your behaviour. Though I gave the reason of prank and booze to my family and the guests, I'm still not convinced. I know it's something. I deserve to know the truth. Tell me what it is."

"Times have changed. You have to fly high. You deserve all the happiness," I chanted.

"I will wait." He said and left leaving me with my palpitations racing. Rima and Ayan took me home and tended me till I was back to myself.

As I immersed myself in the tempting warm waters of the bathtub, surrendering myself to the bubbles, his words echoed in my mind, again and again. What was my heart trying to say to me? Why did I come all the way from Kolkata to Goa? What was happening to my heart? It was speedily distancing itself from the sensible thoughts of my mind. I had just gone there on a mission to save Ranbir from the vulturous girl, but was it also because my heart conspired? I had just called off my wedding, was just pulling away from a traumatized life, how could I aspire and think of a second love life so soon? After a long hour, I decided to go back to Kolkata. It's best to keep myself away from the commotion and troublesome parts of life, I thought. Ranbir would anyway get to know about her very soon. It was his life, not mine. Why should I poke my nose in it? And maybe after all, he knew she was like that and was marrying her after she had confessed and he had forgiven her sins. So why the heck should I interfere in their private matters? It was his life, his choice.

I called Rima to say that I had decided that we'd leave Goa the next day, but I ended up saying – "Plan C".

She called up Ayan, who was on his way from Pune to Goa. He had gone there to meet his cousins. She said that it was time to initiate the third plan.

We had to find Meera's boyfriend in Mumbai who had gifted her the Audi she was using so guiltlessly.

I called Ranbir and, using my social information engineering skills, learned that Meera was travelling to Mumbai again to meet her ailing granny the day after.

I was sure that she was going to meet her boyfriend there. We decided to follow her and crack the mystery.

We bought some *burkhas* for the three of us and hired a car.

Last minute, Rima backed off as she felt feverish and dizzy. But she pushed me to proceed with Ayan.

When Meera reached Mumbai in her car, she entered a flat at Andheri. We also entered cautiously so as to not catch her eye. But the guard stopped us at the gate to enter our details in the register. Ayan wrote down our names as Begum Ramira, Samira.

That moment, only r-s saved us… thanks to our English teachers. Or it didn't. He looked at our similar names in the register and told us to show our faces. Awkwardly, we tried to bribe the guard but he turned out to be upright and honest. As Ayan started fighting with the guard to let us in, saying that we have some lifesaving business to do, the guard became all the more perturbed and started dialling the police. That was when I stopped him and requested to hear our plight and position.

After hearing our hour-long story in his cabin and seeing our identity cards, he seemed to understand we were no criminals but here to conduct a rescue mission. He agreed to support us and so divulged the details we needed.

"Meera madam has come to meet Varun here. He is a very nice guy and so I'm doing this for him. He is such a kind person that he wouldn't hurt a fly," he said. "He has also fixed a marriage date and given the cards for printing. His maid was telling me this yesterday. If I say anything, he may not believe me. So please do something soon," he said with his hands folded near his forehead and worry lines across his brow.

We reached Varun's flat and put our ears to the door to hear any possible sound, but the door was soundproof and we couldn't hear anything. We sat on the stairs in front of his door. We decided to take a video of them when they came out.

Indeed, after two long hours of waiting, they emerged, hand in hand. Meera was in a black tube top and a long silver skirt, Varun in brown cargo pants and a cream t-shirt. It seemed like he was deeply in love as his eyes were only wandering where she went. We filmed their short romantic walk.

We followed them to the restaurant and managed to record them kissing, cuddling, and flirting. We had to tell the manager that we were from a detective agency when we were caught doing this by the staff. We escaped by telling him that this was a marriage verification case. But they were careless to not ask for any identity cards and allow us to continue. But ours was a genuine case, wasn't it? Now that I had seen them both, I understood that whatever Cora had said was right.

Stupendously satisfied with what we had achieved, we returned to our hotel in Mumbai and I sent a text to Ranbir telling him that he needed to come to Mumbai the next morning as it was something urgent and important, in fact critical. On his arrival, we took him directly to Varun's house and rang the bell. We covered the eye-piece on the door with our hands so that Meera wouldn't be able to see us. And lo, she opened the door in a satin night suit.

"Who is it, baby?" Varun emerged and held her.

"Oh, oh!" she was lost for words.

"What the heck. Bloody hell! What's going on?" Ranbir said clearly shocked and walked inside to the living area and sat on the sofa with a hand on his head.

"Oh. Is this any kind of planned surprise?" said Meera in a bid to save herself.

"What surprise. What's happening, Meera? Ranbir? Speak up!" Varun said hovering his eyes at both of them in turns.

Meanwhile a shocked Ayan took Ranbir and Meera to the balcony and they discussed. After their return to the living area, Ranbir broke the staut silence - "I have no answers and I'm sure even Meera doesn't have any say in this."

Then, Ranbir and Meera looked at each other and broke into a hearty laugh. I was shocked. What's happening? Is this now some part of a big ongoing conspiracy? Everyone knowing everything. Am I the only fool here?

"Noya. I don't know what I should do with you," Ranbir said to me.

"Varun and Meera, I apologize on behalf of them. We will come back later for a party. For now, I'm taking them for a drive." He said and we all proceeded out.

Ranbir was still in disbelief so he kept quiet all the while. Ayan excused that he had to leave for Goa as Rima wasn't well and he had to be with her. After he left, it was only both of us – me and Ranbir. We went to a coffee shop as Ranbir wanted shots of caffeine and sugar to pacify his nerves. I got to know something about him; when under pressure, coffee pacified him.

"Now tell me the story. What's the commotion?" He asked me with bated breath.

"How could you take this so casually? Doesn't it matter that your fiancé is with another guy? Moreover, she also has cheated behind your back." I blurted quite insensitively.

"I realize now, why you had come in an inebriated state during the engagement function. You wanted to disrupt it. But you could have simply given me a call and shared all this. Why such complexities. And I'm really hurt thinking about Varun. He is such a nice guy. And thanks to you for playing the role of a friend," he said, looking at me in his usual intense manner.

"My pleasure. A friend in need is a friend indeed," I said smiling.

"I again apologize for that day. Now I understand why you had behaved so cranky and insane," he said.

"Just forget it. I'm sorry that you had to break your engagement with her," I said.

"I had to break off the engagement. Are you kidding me?" He shrieked.

"Haven't I just broken off your relationship with her? Or you still intend to carry on with the relationship with Meera?" I asked.

He stamped his feet on the ground, slammed his cup of coffee on the table and said, "Look Noya. Till now you haven't understood me, and you say I'm your friend."

"I want to know now. What you feel about it?" I insisted.

"Ok mad girl, listen. When did I say that I and Meera were in a relationship?" He whispered.

"You only said you had an engagement function," I snapped.

"But does it mean that any engagement function at my home will be mine? See again, you stuck to your vital nature of jumping to conclusions, overlooking facts. Why are you so judgmental?" he said.

"God. Not again. Don't tell me," I said in agony, realizing the blunder.

"But that day at Eme, you had shared about your mother fixing your marriage with her," I asked weakly.

"Oh that. You went on insisting that she is my fiancée. So I just thought of putting up a prank and stretching it a bit," he said and chuckled.

"Meera was getting engaged to a cousin of mine. But I think you were too dazed out that day to differentiate between the cousin and me," he said.

"I and Meera were never into any relationship. Meera was tying the knot with my cousin and not me. And that cousin is no one else, but Varun. So the accusation that she is cheating on me has been ruled out. And the second accusation that she has cheated Varun by being with Rohan calls for a clarification. I would prefer if you call Rima yourself and ask her. This time without jumping to any conclusion, ask her clear facts. We will talk after your call to her," he said while holding my hand.

As Ranbir waited in the car in the parking bay area and I after the brief talk with Rima, came back and sat drenched in embarrassment, guilt, which was gripping me like hordes of maneater reptiles.

“I’m so sorry Ranbir. I just meant to do good and this happened. God will punish me,” I said and burst into tears.

He held my hand in a tight grip and lifted it and said, “Ask for forgiveness from heart. God never punishes his children. And I just had a talk with Meera. She had forgiven you then and there. She understands why you have done what you have done. So stop harassing yourself. It’s you who is troubling yourself. No one else is bothered about what happened. So stop pondering.”

“Oh God. And all this while I was thinking otherwise.” I raked my hair. “I want to get drunk, Ranbir. My head is bursting with a migraine. I need relief. I want to get away from the thoughts. I need to sink in,” I said.

“Red wine please with fish fillets,” I ordered my part to the server in the bristling and happening pub, thumping with music.

“I have to change. I know I have to,” I said to him.

“Hmm, you don’t have to change; just work on your trait. You are too judgmental. Don’t jump to conclusions without gathering the facts. You were…towards me as well,” he said.

“Yes, I was. I apologize for it. And regarding Meera, just because her first impression on me wasn’t a good one, I presumed it to be her in all that people said. Not even once did I try to clarify or reach the truth as to who was the girl they were talking about. It was Jenny, not Meera,” I said remorsefully.

“Life is all about learning. Don’t be harsh on yourself. Take this as an experience and move on,” he said.

“I wasn’t like this earlier. My earlier relationship turned me into this. I find it so difficult to trust new people now.” I said, made bolder with the liquid I was sipping.

"Share with me. If you want to."

"Not today. Some other day," I said.

We went to a hotel to check-in and asked for two rooms. That was when the receptionist gave us a pamphlet saying we could attend it. It read, "Disco Night" with the city's most popular DJ in the discotheque of the hotel located in the basement.

"Ranbir. Let's go here. I don't want to go to the room and sulk. I want to sink my worries by dancing away." I said, further reading the details.

Before he could answer, I held his hand and soon we were dancing. I danced like never before. I enjoyed like never before. One has to let go if one has to move on.

"Hey Ranbir. Is it really you? Can I trust my aging eyes," said a girl appearing from nowhere and pulling Ranbir towards her.

"Oh my God. Is it you Kokila? How are you? What a pleasant surprise." She nodded and gave him an air kiss and a hug.

"Mind dancing with me?" she asked him.

"I'm not alone here. I have a friend, Noya. Can't leave her alone." He said pointing towards me.

"Oh I understand. Let's sit and talk. We are meeting after so long, honey," she said.

As we sat down and sipped some cocktails, there were questions shot by her.

"Are you in touch with Tanya?" she asked him and I saw his expressions going haywire.

"I was. But she changed her number and email ID. Also blocked me everywhere. I don't know why. You knew that I would have never disturbed her if that's what she wanted." He said and she nodded in approval.

"Even I'm not in touch with her. But I heard she is in Mumbai." She said and then noticing that I was part of the alien discussion, diverted the topic and asked me more about myself. When he left for a while to attend a call, she even asked me whether Ranbir had any feelings for me. She said he is a gem which is hard to find and if I get along into a relationship with him, it will be like an eternal love story.

"So what were you complaining about me?" He returned and interrupted our conversation.

"Yes. All your secrets are out now." She giggled and winked at him. She was at ease with him. She excused herself and left when she got a call from her office that she has to immediately report to work to fix an escalated customer complaint.

"What do they think? That we become their chained goats as long as they pay us. Anyway, the beer which I'm drinking is given to me by them, for my work. So I can't avoid it. Bye both of you. I have to make a move but we will catch up soon." She said and left in a hurry.

"Another drink please," Ranbir asked the bartender, making it his sixth mug, the effect of the name 'Tanya' on him.

"Who is Tanya?" I asked him. A part of me was in a pandemonium. He is my friend and I felt that I have full rights on him, but tonight made me feel that there is another part of his life that I'm not at all aware of.

He didn't make any attempt to ward off the question or hide anything. The intoxication helped him talk openly, which may not have been the way if he was normal. He opened up on his past: he had loved a girl named Tanya in his college. But it didn't work out as she had walked away. Now we were square with each other. He knew my past and I knew his.

It was 2.00 a.m. by the time the club started getting to shut down. We were amongst the last few. For the first time in all the days I had known him, he was most vulnerable today.

"Can't we stay? I don't want to stay alone today?" He spoke in the elevator while I pressed sixth floor.

"But..." I paused.

"I have an idea. Let's go to the terrace. I love sky gazing. I need to feel the fresh air and look at the stars today. I'm in desperate need. Please." He said it in a way that no one on earth could have declined his request.

"But won't the terrace door be locked?" I said.

"Follow me. I know a secret passage. I have used it earlier. Walk fast." He said and led the way.

We jaunted along the corridor, walking past many standard rooms, deluxe suites, then to the staff elevator. There, we directed the lift to the terrace.

"Oh look at that blinking star. It's the brightest. She must be my mom, 'coz I feel she is smiling at me and blessing me." I said, now lying on the floor of the crown of the tall building which stood twenty floors high.

"I'm sure she must have been as beautiful, as kind-hearted and brave as you." He said and his appreciation directed towards me was mystical, made more ritzy with the cool breeze cutting across us.

"Will you also search for me in the sky after I leave the world?" He asked me. He was probably unaware of what he was saying. He was not in his complete senses.

"Yes, I will. Only if I manage to survive that long." I replied.

"And will you search for me after you leave me and go way?" He asked. I shuddered when I heard that.

"Tell me Noya. Will you also leave me heartbroken with a wounded heart? Just like Tanya did. I need to know your response. Speak up." He said and before I replied, I could hear him snorting. I was glad that I had escaped that situation, from not answering his question.

Sunrays woke me up and I opened my eyes clumsily. Ranbir was still sleeping. We had to reach our room before anyone caught our triumph and assumed stuff. It would have been an unimaginably awkward situation if anyone saw us. And telling them that we are room residents would confirm we are insane. Who appreciates wild whacky behaviour, when it's not the self whose doing it. *The world lives with 'When I do it, it's cool; when they do it, it's weird' attitude*.

I shook him to activate his waking up. As soon as he gathered energy, I pulled him till he stood up and we went to our rooms. When we reached, inserted the key cards and went to our respective rooms, I realised that I didn't have any clothes to wear as Ayan had left with my bag in his car. I decided to wear the same dress with no other option.

As I was relaxing in the bath tub, someone rang the door bell. It rang again. I should have hung the 'Do not Disturb' card outside the door. By the time I hurriedly wore the bathrobe and peeped through the eyehole on the door, the one ringing the bell had left. I opened the door and this time, hung the DND card before immersing myself back into the water.

After half an hour, the phone rang.

"Hello, were you asleep? I had come to your room but you didn't open." It was Ranbir.

"Yep. I was in the shower. By the time I opened, you had left." I said.

"Oh I'm extremely sorry to have been a hindrance. Keep a habit of using cards."

"Hmm. I have done that now. Anything urgent?" I said.

"Open the door and take the newspaper in. Read it," he said.

Out of curiosity, I ran to the door and checked. Along with the newspaper pouch, there hung a carry bag on the knob. I took both inside. The carry bag was empty. Just when I was about to throw it on the bed, I noticed a small receipt in it. I opened and read -

'We had tried reaching you for delivery. But we guess you were busy. Please dial 1661 for us to attempt a second time delivery of the goods purchased.'

Who has ordered what! As I feebly dial the number, the lady on the other end asked me to specify what clothes I need. This must be the handiwork of Ranbir and no one else. But I decided to accept the help without any fuss. After all, we are friends. He has rights on me and I have on him. And so he understood my unstated need.

"Thank you," I called him up and said.

"Shut up. And get ready soon. We need to meet Meera and Varun before we leave for Goa," Ranbir said. "As you wanted."

He always bowled me over with each passing day. How he remembered each and every wish of mine. How he understood my nitty gritty unstated needs too.

During the return flight to Goa, out of some extravagant, some simple, some strong, some sweet, some flowery fragrances, one familiar musky smell kept me at ease as he sat next to me. We were close. My mind was now home to a blend of emotions. I felt shivers running through me. Sitting next to him, talking to him was making me tremble for reasons unknown to me. Or did I know the reason?

"I didn't say anything to you that day because it might have harmed your reputation. Everyone would have blamed you for interrupting the event. I hope you understand why I was quiet. But I knew that day itself that it's something you are concerned about. I didn't know what it was, but I trusted you would do it. And you did it." His gaze was getting more intense.

"And it turned out to be a hoax." I said and burst to laughter. We had a hearty roar together.

"Noya, can I tell you something?" His voice suddenly became low-pitched and intense. I knew where it was leading.

"I'm sleepy. I'm off for a nap," I said this and put my ear plugs on and pretended to close my eyes. I did not like confronting his powerful eyes. They had some divine energy in them which always pulled me towards him. I was unprepared. I couldn't have gotten into this.

Before he left the airport, he hugged me tight and whispered into my ears, "I want to say something to you. Earlier I was confused. I was under the effect of my conscience."

"I know what it is, but don't say it," I said this thinking he hadn't exactly said anything but I knew what he was leading up to.

I freed myself from his hug, and ran to the car in which Rima and Ayan were waiting.

"What's happening baby?" Rima chuckled.

"Love is in the air in Goa," Ayan paired up with her to tease me.

"Shut up, guys. It's nothing." I defended myself. It is so strange that when a girl is free and single, these words are magical; if she is committed, they're a whirlpool; if married, they are messy; and if in a messed up mental state, this same love is a nightmare.

❖

'Please meet me. I need to confess a very important matter. I'm dying of guilt here.' My cell phone beeped displaying Ranbir's text.

"Thank God you came here, Noya. My heart was pumping out of its cage. I needed to talk to you so badly," he said while seated at the round wooden table of the restaurant overlooking the sea.

"What is it? And what is so urgent that you made me skip lunch at Samaira's place?" I asked.

"Noya, you may feel offended, get angry or hate me. But I need to share something with you. When I was eighteen, Dad gifted me a new car. I was learning to drive it when one day, I hit an old man. My friends shouted at me to drive away. I was so scared and I was in a dilemma on what to do. Should I listen to my friends and avoid the hassles of the police or listen to my heart and save the man? They said that someone would come and save the man who was now lying unconscious on the road. I knew that no one would turn up and he might die if I didn't take him to the hospital. I took him to the hospital. That was when I realized you must always listen to what your heart says in times of a crisis.

"You know, when the man gained consciousness in the hospital, he said to me: 'Son, when I was falling down on the road after getting hit by your car, I said to God, please forgive this man and please save my life. My family is waiting for me at home. It is my 70th birthday today and I was dying. Save me, God. And God listened to me. And I forgive you because you didn't run away like others we read about or see incidents about. Thank you, my boy.'

"That old man taught me the best lesson of my life: never be afraid of doing something that your heart tells you to, no matter what the consequences. When it's life, don't leave someone who needs you. When others prompt you to run away, stick more strongly to your chosen course and prove them wrong. If I had run away that day, I would have never had a single peaceful night."

As he said this, he kept his cold hand on mine and continued, "After that day, today is the day I feel a similar apprehension. I want to listen to my heart. I want to say that I love you."

I was at a loss of words. My blood was pumping up and down my body, my breath pacing faster, but I knew I couldn't allow myself this relationship. Not yet. I wasn't ready. And he was good a guy. He deserved a better life.

"Ranbir, I have already said this relationship is not possible," I said curtly and got up. "Don't ever contact me."

Saying this I turned and exited the place in haste. Uncontrollable tears flowed down my face during my drive home.

"Hey lady, look out. Don't drive if you are drunk," screamed the truck driver with whom I had just had a narrow escape accident. I halted the car and called Priyanka for a talk. I needed to vent out.

"Hello Nikhil, I'm stressed out. I'm confused," Ranbir said into the phone to his friend.

"What is it? Is it that girl Noya?" asked Nikhil. "Shall I suggest something? Kidnap her and take her away if you feel that she loves you too, but is not saying anything due to societal pressure."

"Will you help?" Ranbir asked.

"You want to kidnap a girl and you need my help? Buddy, all this drama happens only in soaps, plays and movies. There the police are unreal, punishment is chimeral, the consequences unreal. Here, if we get caught, the cops will hit my ass till it turns from wheatish to red. Sorry, man. And can we talk tomorrow? For God's sake, it is 3.00 a.m. I got home just an hour back. I'm drunk," he said, managing to utter the words.

"Bye, Nikhil. I didn't want help with kidnapping someone. Holy God, don't you know me? Can I ever kidnap my love?" Ranbir said and disconnected the call.

"Suraj, I need help." Ranbir dialled another friend of his.

"Dude, you are the most decent, and noble gentleman of our group. Why are you trying to get involved in all these things? Nikhil just called me and told me about your conversation. Are you out of your mind? Don't be mad! Go and sleep, good night."

"Nikhil and Suraj," this time they were on a conference call, "I need help. I won't let you sleep till I get peace. First of all, let me clarify something. I am not planning to kidnap anyone. It was Nikhil who suggested it and then shared it with you, Suraj."

"Nikhil, you ball. Will hit it next time we meet," Suraj ranted at Nikhil.

"Ok, let's meet up. Come home you nutcracks. I will have a shower with cold water and my hangover should go away," Nikhil said.

"Even if it doesn't, I will pinch your ball and make sure the hangover goes away," Suraj said.

A serious discussion began in Nikhil's bedroom.

"So you love a girl?" Suraj said, diving his fingers into the bowl of peanuts while sipping on the can of beer.

"And she is under depression," Nikhil said.

"And you want to stop her from going to Kolkata in the evening tomorrow? Hmm…interesting," Suraj added.

"But you don't know if she loves you," Nikhil said. "Wow wow wow. How filmy! Rascal, I see no sense in it."

"Let's focus on what we have gathered. Ranbir wants to take her to some place where it will be them only. Isn't it better if you just take her to a temple? You have said that she is spiritual and had gone alone on a pilgrimage. So take her there and propose to her. What could be a better place for Noya than a temple?" Suraj suggested.

"I know, but she won't accept it. I know her. She will give me excuses and I will have no answer to them. I have to do this. My idea is to take her to some far off place where it will be only us, away from families, friends, society," Ranbir said.

"Since you are so adamant about being with her, let's do it. But we won't be the frontrunners in this. I will give you the contact details of Gary, a Russian goon. I know a person, whom I met yesterday in the club, who gets smuggled goods from him. He can help. But they are dangerous, and part of the mafia gang. So be cautious, careful and safe. And if the police catches us, the asses they beat shouldn't be ours, but yours buddy. Promise us that," Nikhil paused. "But if needed, we will give our asses for you."

"Oh God. Not again. Nikhil, are you still under the effect of alcohol after your bloody cold bath? Come to your senses. I just need ideas about where I can find a private space where just the the two of us can be," Ranbir said.

The trio lay down on the bed, facing the swiftly rotating fan, and discussed the available options.

"Option 1: The moon, Mars – all that would mean getting NASA involved which would take too much time and we would have to deal with and confront legal and cross country hassles," said Nikhil, trying hard to keep his eyes open. Every time he shut them, Sooraj pinched his balls.

"Option 2: The ocean – We both could dive into it, talk and I propose to her there. But what if she has hydrophobia," Ranbir said.

"Option 3: Book a chartered plane and fly high in the skies. But you guys won't have privacy – the pilot and the attendant would be there," said Nikhil drowsily. And before he heard the response, he dozed off. He was not to be blamed for he did try his best to keep himself awake. Suraj spared him this time.

"Option 4: The Himalayas. But what if she has fear of heights?" Ranbir said.

"Option 5: Antartica. Again, a lot of preparation time would be required," Suraj said and the next moment, he screamed, "Man, oh jerk! How come the Himalayas not hit my head this long? I was there last year. Go there! That's the best. All set and done. Now let's sleep."

Before Ranbir could think of another option, he gathered that the fourth option was the best, most feasible, approachable, and sensible one. But he needed further information and Noya's acceptance as well for the plan to go forward. So the next day, he planned to meet her and asked her out. She agreed reluctantly.

As he sat in the pub which was overly decorated in red, there came a man, dressed in a white coat and black pants with spiked red hair, "Sir, do you want to order something before your company drops in? You have been waiting for an hour."

"No, not now. I would wait for some more time before I order anything," he said while twiddling uncomfortably in the chair, wondering whether he should do what he was planning to do. But then he remembered her face, her smile, her eyes, her voice. He decided that he has to do it.

He opened the folder which Suraj and he had prepared the previous night and checked out the details which comprised her name, physical attributes, address and so on, which was required for the trek. Alongside, he also checked the prerequisites for the trek – one of the check items stated was a mandatory medical fitness approval certificate from a doctor. He had not thought of that till now. What if she had some medical problem and was unable to join him on the trek? How could he make such a plan? He had learnt all this in his management course. Plans have to be made considering all resources, risks, contingencies and targets. But again, visualizing her face in his mind assured him that he would manage it.

He reclined in the chair and began to think. Why was she refusing to admit that she loved him? He had seen it in her eyes that she cared for him. He wanted to ask her the same when she would be away from the world, where her decisions wouldn't be manipulated by worldly factors. So he had to take her away from her world. *Breaking Free.*

His thoughts were interrupted by the sound of footsteps and a flowery fragrance and without even looking up, he knew that it was her. This is the power of love. His heart smiled. He smiled in relief that she has arrived.

"Sorry Ranbir. I thought I would not come, but then I came. Tell me fast, whatever it is. And don't repeat what you have told me earlier. You know the response," I said, not looking into his eyes. But at that point of time, I was holding my hands tightly and trying to contain the underlying emotions I had for Ranbir. I was trying my best to hold back my tears and behave like a cold human being. But I knew it was for the better of both.

"Okay, look here. I have two registration forms for the Himalayan trek. I'm not forcing you. But before you go to Kolkata, I want us to spend some time together. And I remember what you told me earlier – that once in your life, you want to travel to the Himalayas. So now is the time. Please don't deny," he coaxed me.

"See, after all that I have suffered, I was pretending that nothing hurts me. I was behaving like a normal girl who is happy, but that doesn't mean I will accept anyone after all that I have endured. Ask my heart how I'm suffering now. Even if it starts liking someone, I have to put that extra thrust to stop it. I have to avoid, ignore, and crush all the feelings I have in me. I can't start any new relationship as I'm not ready for it," I said while sipping some water from the mineral water bottle kept on the table. In my mind, I thought the situation was no different. The only change was that this time, it was a guy I liked and admired.

"I'm leaving this evening. And dare you follow me. These days, I'm toiling day and night for my NGO. The students are doing well in academics and vocational courses. They are even winning many contests and competitions," I said.

"Ok, but take the form at least. Just in case you change your mind." He said tirelessly. My refusals, denials never tired him.

"Fine. I will think about it. I can't postpone my Kolkata plan. I have to go there. I'm opening a branch there. If I plan to join the trek, I will be there. If you don't hear from me, please take it as a final no for an answer," I said this while taking the form.

Ranbir drove back to his house, unable to control his emotions, his apprehensions, his tension, his desires, his tears, and his love. He had planned the Himalayan trip as he wanted to spend some time with her. He was not yet ready to let her go. Above everything, there was a bond of friendship. He would have never done the planning if he felt that she didn't love him. It was so not like him.

'What has love done to me? I'm in love with her. Nowadays, my thoughts just start and end with her. I just need to know what she thinks and really wants. If she tells me once that she doesn't love me, I will never disturb her again," Ranbir thought.

Ranbir packed his bags ticking off everything in the checklist printed on the form. He opened the brochure which was very inviting and exciting in vivid colors.

He had not slept the night before the start of the tour as there were feelings of doubt, and apprehension engulfing him every now and then. All his calls and messages to Noya went unanswered.

He wasn't sure whether he should go on the trek. She was not responding. But the excursion was necessary. She needed to break free from her past, from her barriers, from her world to decide her future life. She was too tangled up in societal pressures, worldly webs and emotional nets.

He caught the flight and reached Delhi. He switched on the phone when he landed; still there was no response. He started to panic. He, however, decided to continue.

Tring. Tring.

His heart nearly leapt out of his body when he heard the phone ringing. But it was his parents calling. He took a deep breath and said to himself, "Move on Ranbir. Keep going. Keep moving." This action calmed him down. As he walked past two fat and short policemen, he stumbled over someone's luggage and fell down. Love makes you stupid and careless at times.

He reached Haridwar and checked into a hotel while waiting for the next bus, or was it to fetch him some time till he got some response. After a long wait, he picked up his rucksack, paid the cashier and waited in front of the travel agent's office. He drank hot tea from the small stall opposite the office and felt that it had come to the end. The end before it had even begun. She has not responded to a single text. He was devastated. He hadn't expected this. He knew she also liked him. She had wanted to come to the Himalayas. She had shared her desire with him. He looked up, past the dilapidated roof of the office. There stood the majestic Himalayas – brown, green, white, unmovable, strong, determined, capped with white snow and having the blessings of the clear blue sky and the sunlight above. Though he thought many times of going back to Goa, the view had an impact that made his soul, his heart, his mind, his legs want to go nowhere else. So he decided to proceed for the trek without her. It would break him free from his own emotional trap. On the peak, he would seek peace and strength from the Almighty and thank Him for watching over the one whom he loved so much. It was a wondrous thing that in such a short spell of time, she had become an integral part of him.

"It is all right. Not all love stories are meant to have happy endings. I must be happy with what makes her happy. If she feels she won't be happy with me, then it's fine. All I want is her happiness…wherever she is…whoever she will be with," he told himself.

He reached the base station, Uttarkashi and informed his family and friends, one text out of which was also sent to Noya, that he would be out of reach for seven days as no cell tower was capable of giving a strand of signal in the vast mountains as he would climb. He went to the registration counter and registered himself, following which he received a brochure containing the schedule for the next seven days. He looked at it with widened eyes. The routine looked quite exciting. His gymming habits would definitely help. The only problem he had was –

"Wake up at 5.00 a.m.! Are you kidding me? Should I go on this trip after all? Will I be able to manage everything along with the emotional baggage?" He asked himself.

Yes you can, a voice deep down inside encouraged him. "I can. I will," he said while entering the numbered tent he was allotted.

He looked at the Day 1 schedule.

Time	**Programme**
05:30 - 05:50 am	Morning tea
06:30 - 07:30 am	Acclimatization training & stretching exercise
07:45 - 08:30 am	Breakfast
08:30 - 09:15 am	Administrative talk & group division
09:20 - 09:45 am	Introduction with the participants
09:50 -10:30 am	Tips on rucksack packing
10:45 - 12:30 pm	Ice breaker game
12:30 - 02:00 pm	Lunch break
02:00 - 02:45 pm	Briefing & demo on improvised shelter-making & field cooking.
03:00 - 04:15 pm	Environmental game
04:15 - 04:45 pm	Tea
04:45 - 05:30 pm	Debriefing
05.30 - 06.30 pm	Know Your Leadership Style
06:30 - 07:30 pm	Dinner
07:30 - 08:30 pm	Screening of 'First Indian woman to climb Everest'
09:00 pm	Lights out

He was so tired and drained that he slept without any sense that night. He looked forward to the next day - Day 1.

"Morning tea!" shrieked the monstrous lady. It is amazing how the sweetest of the sweet people seem like ruthless monsters when they wake you up early in morning.

"Let me sleep some more. I wake up at seven in the morning every day. I will feel drowsy and cranky the whole day if I don't get my hours of sleep," he managed to mumble and closed his eyes.

"Sleep! Have you come all this way to nap? Then son, you should have gone on a vacation to a resort and not a trek. Here – this will help you sleep." She splashed freezing water on his face.

"What the hell you are doing, lady?" He woke up in shock. His head drenched wet and dripping with cold water. He felt like his body was being pierced with knives. As he wiped the droplets of the deathly water from his eyelashes and eyes, he realized that right in front of him was *Madam Pal,* the first Indian woman to scale Mount Everest. He had a chapter on her in his school books and after he had read that, he was completely awesmitten by her. She was his idol since then. His mouth seemed stuck with strong glue. He was left with no words. He was gobsmacked. After some moments, when the feeling had sunk in, he greeted her, bowing his head down to apologize. He realized that in the Himalayas, no money, no fame, no personality can overpower the power of the mountains. It is only you along with your willpower and determination that can help you survive.

"Sorry, Ma'am. And I can't believe it is you standing right in front of me. I have read about you in books, on the internet, and in the news," he said.

"Hello, my boy. And if I had slept like you, I would never have climbed the Everest. Improve your five senses, trust your sixth sense, strengthen your mind and body. To climb a mountain, you have to be fit and strong. And put on your number tag. No one remembers names in these vast mountains. We remember only numbers," she said. "Ah D2, is it?"

"I understand, Ma'am. I will. And can I take a selfie with you?" He said, bringing out the kid inside him. He took a selfie with his zero-signal phone. That photograph which he would cherish all his life.

The man who distributed tea was a very serious-looking man, covered entirely in woollens except for his eyes. They were covered with goggles.

As he drank tea, he got the next announcement. "Come here for the acclimatization training and stretching exercise," roared the trainer.

He drank the remaining hot tea in a swig, burnt his throat and ran to the exercise area where six people were already doing the demonstrated exercise. They were his fellow trek-mates.

"Where is your partner, D2?" yelled the trainer.

"She didn't come," he said with a heavy heart.

"Alright. Now get going. Rotate your waist. Fast, fast, fast. Haven't you had your tea?" screamed the trainer.

He had booked for the couple trekking programme, and there were four couples that were supposed to train for the trek. With Noya missing, that made a total of seven of them.

After having noodles for breakfast, the participants were given some administrative advice, taught types of signals for emergency, for danger, for recreation and so on, shared how to answer nature's calls during trekking and so on. They were also introduced to each other.

"Hello, we are A1 and A2. We have been married for a year and we're from Pune. We both work with Maersk logistics. We want to strengthen our bond through this trek."

"Hello, we are B1 and B2. We have been married for thirty years and are from Delhi. We want to reignite our relationship and memories through this trek."

"Hello, we are C1 and C2. We have been living in together for two years and come from Mumbai. We want to commit to our relationship and so we came here to be with each other before deciding for the big day."

"Hello, I am D2. D1 hasn't joined me. I'm from Goa and I'm here to reawaken and strengthen myself." He concluded the introduction, after which they also shared their real names.

Day One concluded with games, inspirational video sessions, and basic lessons on dos and don'ts.

The obvious love between all the couples warmed him in the chilly weather. Seeing them, he missed Noya all the more. Love was in the air. Only that his love was not present with him, physically.

Time	**Programme**
05:30 - 05:50 am	Morning tea
06:30 - 07:15 am	Breakfast
07:15 - 07:30 am	Tips on Mountain manners / hill walking
07:30 -01:00 pm	Village visit
01:00 - 02:30 pm	Lunch break
02:30 - 03:00 pm	Briefing on point to point march & Orienteering
03:00 - 05:00 pm	Point to point march exercise
05:00 - 06:00 pm	Debriefing (tea in between)
06:30 - 07:30 pm	Dinner
07:30 - 08:30 pm	Slide show / Camp fun
09:00 pm	Light out

"Wake up! Wake up!" the voice screamed.

"Let me sleep for a little while longer, please," he said and put his head under the pillow so that he could save it this time.

Swish! This time the water fell on his body. As he got up, he stared in disbelief – standing in front of him was his damsel.

"Noya! You have come. You don't know how much I missed you." He cried as he embraced her in a quick hug. He pinched his belly hard to make sure it was not some dream or hallucination, which were quite common due to lack of sleep.

"If my mornings are going to be like this, with you waking me up, I don't mind the chilled weather or the water," Ranbir said to me while combing his hair with his fingers.

"Madam Pal told me to wake you up in that fashion. And I felt good doing that," I said sounding cruel.

But Ranbir thought – *'For you, I'm ready to do and face anything.'*

"So what made you come back here?" He asked me while we sat together on the wooden planks and sipped tea.

"First I thought I wouldn't come. But then I told myself – baby, this is not just a trip to any other place – it is one to the mighty Himalayas. I looked at the form again. As soon as I did that, I saw the brochure for the trek. The brochure was so tempting that I came for the mountains. So don't have any expectations. I'm here only for the mountains," I said this while controlling the emotions, as I could see tears of happiness in his eyes on seeing me. My eyes were also wet.

During the village trip, we experienced rural life. The inhabitants in the huts were overtly creative – they wore colourful blouses and skirts, men and women alike, with beautiful handmade jewellery. We interacted with them and played games as well.

I was an expert at rock-climbing and trekking as I had been an active trekker in my school days. After the long day, I realized at bedtime that we had been assigned the same tent – this being a couples' trekking programme.

"You sleep there and I will sleep here," I had distanced my bed from his and placed it near the soft door of the tent, away from the heat of the lamp which was near his bed.

"No, you sleep here and I will sleep there," he said, swapping places with me. He wanted me to be warm. I slept without another word.

Ranbir too went off to sleep. He had realized that she had indeed come for the trek only.

Day 3

For the twelve-kilometre trek to Morsona which was at a height of 7,500 feet, we took along our packed lunches and field cooking equipment and tents. After reaching the camp, we began to cook for the supper and pitch our tents.

It was amazing to walk with him towards the mountain peaks. We had two cane sticks to support the walking. We kept clambering and climbing. At times, I had to hold his hand when I got tired. And at times, he held mine. After a while, it had become an unspoken, unstated requirement which repeated at intervals. And hand in hand, we walked with a better determination

For Ranbir, these were the happiest moments of his life. The one whom he loved was with him, together exploring a heavenly mountain.

We soon came across patches of snow on some parts of the mountain – like white hair on a balding man. I picked some up and threw it at him. He didn't throw back. His eyes didnt move away from me for even a fleeting second. I felt warmth in the cold weather.

Few steps away, Ranbir stood and thought, "I just love seeing my chirping and dazzling princess. She takes my breath away. Can't these days stay with me forever? Can't she be mine forever?"

On reaching Morsona, we started pitching our tents, as had been demonstrated at the base camp, and ate the supper we had prepared and stored earlier. We had potato soup, noodles and two pieces of bread each. At night, I made both our beds near the lamp in a V shaped formation.

"Both have equal rights to get warmth. No gender discrimination or claim of gender rights here," I joked and dozed off.

Ranbir could not sleep the whole night. He read a book on his iPad to pass his time, tossed and turned the remaining time. He controlled his urge to wake her up and talk and talk. But she lay under the heavy blanket which hid her body and face.

Day 4

He was not woken up with chilling water but a warm touch which he decided then and there, as the most memorable moment of his life, to be cherished in his memories in upcoming life.

We climbed ten kilometres uphill to Morapada which was located at 9,500 feet above sea level – encountering spectacular views of the mountain above us, birds hovering over us up above in the pale foggy sky, and more snow on the mountains. It seemed the balding man had used some hair implants and improved the health of his hair.

The soothing sounds of the still mountains, the humming of the bees, the sound of the chirping birds – everything had an enchanting touch to it. The sounds were divine. It was equally intoxicating to stand in the fresh, pristine air of the mighty mountains. Wherever you turned your eyes, you would get breathless, panoramic views of deep ravines, waterfalls, snow and endless greenery. It was picturesque, just like directly out of some edited blockbuster movie.

Day 5 and Day 6

As we walked past Gujjar Hut mountain milestone, standing tall at 10,200 ft, we pitched our tent. It was supposed to be our camping site for the next two days. We had noodles again as it was easier to cook and digest at that altitude.

Ranbir had also got into the habit of waking up daily at 4.30 a.m. This is the impact such adventurous trips have on one. They teach you how to live the right way. They make you realize there is a life in life!

In the evening, we lit a campfire and sat around it – all the four couples. We danced while humming songs, played antakshari, played truth or dare. That was when the other couples coerced Noya and Ranbir to dance together. For her, she was dancing with someone who was her friend, one who charmed her and impacted her life. For him, this was another breath-taking, blissful moment. Her childish chuckles which were long forgotten by her, were spread all over. Her face glittered in the shining moonlight.

That night, even she kept awake till late. She asked him to narrate his memories of life to her. She was not stopping and wanted to know more and more. Ranbir wanted to sit beside her, hug her tight, kiss her lips, caress her nape but he controlled his emotions. In the coldness, his surreptitious feelings were even more vehement. He adjusted the blanket and his seating place so as not to let her know what was running in his mind and body.

The next day, we proceeded towards Surya Top, the peak of this mountain at 13,550 ft, seven kilometres from the camp. We didn't have to carry our luggage as we could keep it in our tents in Gujjar Hut.

"Noya, we only have two days. And after this, you will forget me," he said not looking up into my eyes, while walking hand in hand.

"Not again. Don't start this again. Let us reach the peak of this mountain," I said. "Keep your mouth shut. Don't forget what we have come here for," I said and let his hand go before moving forward.

While walking, I did not notice and stumbled on a small rock.

"Noya," he ran and caught me, saving me from a hard fall. "I had seen the rock yet could not tell you as my mouth was shut." he joshed.

"Okay. While I was toppling, I was falling without any worry as I knew you would be there to catch me," I said.

"Can't we have this moment forever Noya." He said with me leaning on his hand, looking up at him, my hair falling through the gaps of his fingers. We looked at each other for quite a long time, till A1 and A2 came by and A1 knocked on Ranbir's shoulder with his cane stick. "Romance later, bro. We have to return before nightfall. Get going."

We returned to normalcy with the intrusion and soon reached the peak.

On reaching the peak of the mountain, Ranbir shouted my name and it returned with ripples and echoes. Then he said to me, "I couldn't climb Everest, the tallest mountain in the world, but I assume this is the peak of the world because you and I are together."

I felt oblivious with him alongside. His smell, his voice, his glances were causing tumultuous effect in me as well. But I distracted myself and looked away.

"Yoo hoo! Thank you, mighty mountains because you have just made me realize something!" I screamed joyously at the top of my voice.

"What did you realize?" He asked.

"I realized that in the world we all are just travellers. But in life, we try to behave like someone else. You know, like someone our parents want us to be, how our friends want us to be, how our society, how our books want us to be. In this vicious circle, somewhere we lose ourselves and forget who we really are, what we want, where we want to lead ourselves. See these mountains, they are the mighty beings. They live how they want. That is why we salute them. They stand in integrity through time." Ranbir found these words resplendent; he felt the real Noya was back.

"First an irritant, then an unknown stalker, then a known stalker, then an irritant friend, then a good friend and now a..." she paused. "Wow, how soon you change your status! You have it in you, Ranbir. You have goodness oozing out of you. Like some chocolaty filling in a cupcake," I said while pushing my hands into the pockets of my jacket. "You are so warm, so good and so charming," I concluded.

"Noya, can we talk...?" but he was interrupted.

"Ranbir, please don't say it again. Let's go back," I said. If I would have looked into his jeering eyes for another second, I would have ended melting into his arms. But I knew it couldn't be this way.

On reaching Goa airport, Noya wanted to visit the beach as she said she wanted to see the waves. She requested him to accompany her. She sent the driver who had come to pick them up and said that she wanted to drive the car herself.

He remained quiet as he was deeply perturbed and at a loss of words. The thought of her leaving the place was biting him. He didn't know how would he be able to bring his life back to originality. By now, he so much in love with this girl. His days and nights were only peaceful with her thoughts. But he also knew, that love which is forced is not true love. So he put on his sun farer to hide the tears which by now had erupted on his eyes.

"Wait, don't get off the car. I have something to say," she said. Her words had a pulling force in them. Like magnets pull iron.

Unexpectedly, she came towards him, pulled him close to her, enclosed him in a hug and touched her forehead to his, closed her eyes and spoke:

"Here, I imagine myself away from the world, worldly worries, and away from your eyes. I want to tell you something."

"I love you."

She finally said it through her trembling lips.

He kept silent for a long time. He didn't believe what just happened. Was it a dream? Was it a hangover, though he had not consumed any alcohol the previous day. When he looked into her charismatic eyes again, he realized it was reality. Very real. What should he do? Should he jump, should he fly through the seamless, never ending skies? He did not believe what he had just heard from her.

Ranbir got off the car and held her hand. He looked up at the blue sky over the sea and shouted at the top of his voice: "Thank you, God, wherever you are. I love you. I love her and she loves me."

He was beaming with ecstasy, seeing her so joyful and aglow with happiness.

He bent down, took out a twig ring which he had made during the trek and asked her those coveted magical words: "Will you marry me, my princess?"

"Yes, I will," she said with tears rolling down her cheeks and came to him with a leap of faith.

"And calling someone princess is old-fashioned. Nowadays, in this democratic world, princesses are no longer prestigious. Parliamentarians are."

"A lame joke," he retorted. "But you are my princess, any day. Even with your wrinkles and eye bags, you will remain my princess after many many years."

"Ok now. I want to share something before I carry this relationship further," he said.

"Is it about your past relationships?" she asked.

"Yes. But before you arrive at a judgment, please be quiet for ten minutes and hear me out," he said.

"Go on."

"Noya. I'm confused with my feelings. I want to be honest with you."

Then suddenly a wave of water splashed on his face and he got drowned.

"What the hell! Nikhil, is it you?" Ranbir said, perplexed by the sudden turn of events which ended in utter dismay.

"Yes. I had to throw water at you, nutcrack. You have been sleeping like a dead dog for hours. But I threw water only after you were sleep talking and repeating Noya's name." Nikhil said, justifying his act.

"Oh no. Don't tell me that all this was a dream. It can't be." Ranbir cried.

"My boy, the earlier you realize, the better for you. After you both reached the airport, she bid bye and departed. Don't be a fucking bastard and behave like a leech. Let her live. Hasn't she suffered enough and now you too are after her. She doesn't love you man. Understand it." Nikhil said popping his eyes into the sports magazine he held in his hand.

Buzz... There was a constant vibration of Ranbir's phone. There were calls from Noya. He realized that what he had seen till now was just a dream. Noya and he had parted from the airport. They never did come together. All that he saw was just a visualization in his mind, which he really wanted it to be true.

'Come to the railway station at 4.00 p.m.' Noya's latest text message read.

"Ok." He replied. On reaching the railway station, he saw her standing in front of the entrance.

"What is it? Why do you want to meet me here?" He asked, panting and reaching where she stood.

"I have a surprise for you." She said with a glint in her eyes.

"What?" He gasped and coughed. He had flu and it wearied him all the more.

"Turn away and look around at me only when I ask you to," she said.

"Ok now you can turn," she said.

And that turn of his life proved to be the biggest turning point for him. His confusion was now cleared. A super surprise which he might not have thought to ever come true.

"Tanya. Don't tell me it's really you. Where did you disappear? I called you so many times. You never responded. You just left me." He ran in disbelief and hugged Tanya. He then ran to Noya, held her hand and said to her, "You are an angel, Noya. I have no other words for you. Love you for this. You have lead me on the right track."

"How is your modelling job going? I do see you on billboards and advertisements," he said excitedly.

"Ranbir, you had changed all your phone numbers and mail IDs when I tried contacting you. I tried contacting you, but in vain. After a while, I thought I should let it be. But that was till Noya contacted me a few days back and asked me about my feelings towards you. I love you Ranbir. I shouldn't have broken up before pursuing my dreams. It was my fault. Any dream if achieved with the loved one, makes it more glamorous and joyous. I understood it later, but it was too late by then," Tanya said emotionally.

I excused myself and walked away, giving them space and privacy for their long due talks, not before I gave him a hug and put something in his shirt pocket. He read it later when he was back home.

Ranbir,

Our relationship started with arguments but gradually the bud sprung into a beautiful flower, a strong bond of friendship. I'm fortunate enough to have met you. I understand you do get attracted to people whom you like to be around with. At some point of time, I felt it too, but soon realized that it is because you are such a nice person. A person like you is hard to find. And now that I have you, I always want to keep you with me as a friend. You deserve all the happiness in the world. And your world will be complete with Tanya. Above all, above everything is true love. Such love never dies, no matter how many misunderstandings rust it, no matter how much distance comes within. In the heart of it, that love simmers. I don't believe in the concept that love happens only once. There is love in abundance – in family, lover, friends. Even strangers help each other out for the love of humanity. It's on us how to immerse ourselves in it. Tanya still loves you and she has realized her mistake. Accept her back if you can. For love only gets stronger with realizations, forgiveness and time.

Thanks for giving me confidence and a new meaning to my life.

If you are wondering how I found out about Tanya and you, it was the night in Mumbai when you were so drunk that you shared your feelings for Tanya. You told me that you were family friends since childhood but that was only in college that you proposed to her. I got to know that day how you both fell in love, how you planned your wedding and how she walked away as she chose other priorities in life. I think you may not remember that night, as you were too drunk, but you had also shown me her photograph, and told me that you still miss her. You also shared that you should have tried getting her back once more. But she had sent a message that she didn't want you to disturb her life. I searched for her on social network and contacted her, and requested her to meet you. I'm glad that I stopped every time you wanted to propose, so you needn't be guilty. And always remember one thing in life -

We may fail at times in what we do. But it's better than not trying and living forever with the 'what if I had tried' feeling. Failing is not fatal – we do learn, evolve and come out much stronger, experienced and skilled.

Noya
Forever your friend

Epilogue

On her flight to Kolkata, Noya was writing a poem on her tablet when she was interrupted –

"Dear, do you mind exchanging seats. You see, we both are together and this is the first time my wife is travelling in a plane, so she would love to have a window seat. Mine is the middle seat in the row behind." The frail looking old man requested.

"Sure sir. Why not? And enjoy your flight ma'am. Don't forget to take some photographs as memory of your first flight," she said.

After sitting on the new allotted seat, the couple came again and asked her to take her original window seat as someone else had exchanged seats with them.

After she returned to the original seat, a man came and sat to Noya's right, on the middle seat of the row. An hour into the flight, she was engrossed in a magazine when he messed her dress by tripping a can of orange juice over it.

"Oh God ! How can you be so careless?" she screamed.

"I'm extremely sorry. Here, let me wipe it for you." He burst out while handing over some tissue papers to her.

The air hostess noticed this and came running frantically. "We apologize to you Ma'm. You see, we shared with this gentleman that there were passengers travelling by air for the first time and this gentleman wanted to exchange his business class seats with them so that they enjoy their first flight. So he made the couple have his seat along his manager's. Perhaps he is not used to less space in the flight, that's why the callous act."

"And how does this relate to the spill? I'm prone to cold and flu. I'm sure to get one if I sit like this. Anyway, it's ok. I understand," she said while cleaning the white palazzo pant which now had messy blobs of orange juice.

"I'm feeling so uneasy over what happened. If you don't mind, I have a jeans, new and unworn. Please wear that." He said in guilt.

"No it's fine," she said.

"Ok. In case you are thinking that I'm a stranger and it will be awkward wearing my clothes, let me introduce myself to you. I'm a budding struggling actor. Have you heard of Bobby Kapoor? I'm his son. I was in Goa to attend a family function. And now I am going to Kolkata for a photo shoot for the audition of a debut movie," he said in a voice as sweet as honey. It wouldn't be difficult for him to get his way, considering the good looks, fine physique and refined behaviour. He was a dazzling and handsome man in his twenties with shoulder length straight hair. His face was glowing, his features perfect from every angle.

"Please wear my jeans, else I will be at unrest." He said, his eyes so charismatic that denial could not be considered.

"Ok, I will, if you insist. And you are the son of Bobby Kapoor, that famous actor. I have grown up watching his movies. Astonishing and commendable actor. And I will take the jeans on one condition. I will return a new pair to you in Kolkata. Same brand; same model," she said.

He nodded and handed over his contact card. It read 'Harsh Kapoor' and had his phone number. Her mind cracked a joke in mind that how can this Harsh be harsh. Why do parents give such double meaning names to their children. He is such a soft spoken person.

"What's your name ? Have we met before? I'm getting this bizarre feeling that we have. Do you remember?" he said.

"I'm Noya. And this is the first time we are meeting," she replied, absolutely sure that she had not met him earlier. She dozed off the next moment as she was lost.

And she travelled the rest of the flight wearing his jeans, the proposal which she could not deny to relieve him from his guilt.

Recommended Reading

When the Heavens Smiled

Ritesh Arora

Sarthak meets Sarangi through a common friend and love blossoms. But when things seem to be falling on track, like a bolt from the blue, Sarangi is diagnosed with a medical condition that leaves her with only three months to live. With no visible solution at hand, nothing but fate seems to be holding power. Explore uncharted realms of life and beyond with Sarthak as he takes it upon himself to alter Sarangi's destiny.

Ritesh is an author and columnist and works as a management consultant with a global business consulting firm.

ISBN: 978-9382665526; Price: ₹ 195/-; Pages: 168; Binding: Paperback.

You are the Best Wife

Ajay Pandey

This is a story of two people with contradictory ideologies who fall in love. This is a true inspiring story of the author and his struggle with life, after his beloved wife left him halfway through their journey. This heart-warming tale of a boy and a girl who never gave up on their love in face of adversities, ends on a bittersweet and poignant note as Ajay comes to terms with the biggest lesson life has to offer.

An engineer by degree, Ajay works in the IT field and loves to read and trek. He has immortalized his life story through this book.

ISBN: 978-9382665540; Price: ₹ 175/-; Pages: 248; Binding: Paperback.

Keeping the Promises

Dhruv Gajjar

Dhruv had almost lost himself when M brought him back to life with her promises. Dying from a dreadful tumour, every night before they went to sleep, she took a portion of his heart and soul as promises. For better or worse, he'd have to keep the promises for the rest of his life. What were those amusing, surprising and painful promises he kept? Can you live and die…both at the same time?

Dhruv is a doctor by profession, and passionate about working on his fitness using advanced bodyweight training and all kinds of sports.

ISBN: 978-9382665519; Price: ₹ 195/-; Pages: 200; Binding: Paperback.

Love on 3 Wheels

Anurag Anand

A young and ambitious girl misplaces a parcel carrying a large amount of cash. She doesn't want to take help from her suitor who seems to have a whole lot of skeletons in his closet. She doesn't want to lose her job either. What can she do?

This is a saga of love, lust, aspirations and trickery that unfolds over a period of three days, propelling those in its midst into an unmindful frenzy.

Anurag holds a Master's degree in business, but loves to read and explore new places. He has ten books to his credit.

ISBN: 978-9382665588; Price: ₹ 175/-; Pages: 168; Binding: Paperback.

Guru with Guitar

Vikrmn: (CA Vikram Verma)

In spite of his great job and hefty pay package, Viktor didn't feel the sense of contentment. Then he met Kim, his lady luck. This story is his journey through life-changing experiences in India and USA – ranging from writing his first book to becoming a coach for cancer patients, and then a motivational speaker, to finally becoming the Guru with Guitar. The book has 11 heart touching songs, 8 lovely poems and 111 life-changing quotes scripted by the author.

Vikrmn: is a multi-talented person with a knack for numbers, chalk carving, oil painting, spreadsheet programming, photography and obviously, guitar.

ISBN: 978-9382665533; Price: ₹ 250/-; Pages: 264; Binding: Paperback.

A Silent Promise

Namrata Gupta

Avantika's rose tinted glasses grow hazy as she steps into college with a broken heart. She is instantly surrounded with a whole lot of drama from people around her. But slowly, the DU campus life charms her and makes her forget the suffering from her past, especially by bringing her to her soulmate Keith. Everything seems fine, till her nightmare comes to haunt her in real life.

Namrata is a management student with a degree in literature. She loves travelling, exploring new things, and wishes to leave an everlasting impression with her writing.

ISBN: 978-9382665496; Price: ₹ 175/-; Pages: 168; Binding: Paperback.